MW01632341

SEARCHING FOR ODESSA (SPECIAL FORCES: OPERATION ALPHA)

FALLPORT RESCUE OPERATIONS
BOOK SIX

JEN TALTY

PRAISE FOR JEN TALTY

"*Deadly Secrets* is the best of romance and suspense in one hot read!" *NYT Bestselling Author Jennifer Probst*

"A charming setting and a steamy couple heat up the pages in a suspenseful story I couldn't put down!" *NY Times and USA today Bestselling Author Donna Grant*

"Jen Talty's books will grab your attention and pull you into a world of relatable characters, strong personalities, humor, and believable storylines. You'll laugh, you'll cry, and you'll rush to get the next book she releases!" Natalie Ann USA Today Bestselling Author

"I positively loved *In Two Weeks*, and highly recommend it. The writing is wonderful, the story is fantastic, and the characters will keep you coming back for more. I can't wait to get my hands on future installments of the NYS Troopers series." *Long and Short Reviews*

"*In Two Weeks* hooks the reader from page one. This is a fast paced story where the development of the romance grabs you emotionally and the suspense keeps you sitting on the edge of your chair. Great characters, great writing, and a believable plot that can be a warning to all of us." *Desiree Holt, USA Today Bestseller*

"*Dark Water* delivers an engaging portrait of wounded hearts as the memorable characters take you on a healing journey of love. A mysterious death brings danger and intrigue into the drama, while sultry passions brew into a believable plot that melts the reader's heart. Jen Talty pens an entertaining romance that grips the heart as the colorful and dangerous story unfolds into a chilling ending." *Night Owl Reviews*

"This is not the typical love story, nor is it the typical mystery. The characters are well rounded and interesting." *You Gotta Read Reviews*

"*Murder in Paradise Bay* is a fast-paced romantic thriller with plenty of twists and turns to keep you guessing until the end. You won't want to miss this one..." *USA Today bestselling author Janice Maynard*

This book is a work of fiction. Names, characters, places, and incidents are products of the author's imagination or used fictitiously. Any resemblance to actual events or locales or persons living or dead is entirely coincidental.

© 2025 ACES PRESS, LLC. ALL RIGHTS RESERVED

No part of this work may be used, stored, reproduced or transmitted without written permission from the publisher except for brief quotations for review purposes as permitted by law. Without in any way limiting the author's [and publisher's] exclusive rights under copyright, any use of this publication to "train" generative artificial intelligence (AI) technologies to generate text is expressly prohibited. The author reserves all rights to license uses of this work for generative AI training and development of machine learning language models.
This book is licensed for your personal enjoyment only. This book may not be re-sold or given away to other people. If you would like to share this book with another person, please purchase an additional copy for each recipient. If you're reading this book and did not purchase it, or it was not purchased for your use only, please purchase your own copy.

Dear Readers,

Welcome to the Special Forces: Operation Alpha Fan-Fiction world!

If you are new to this amazing world, in a nutshell the author wrote a story using one or more of my characters in it. Sometimes that character has a major role in the story, and other times they are only mentioned briefly. This is perfectly legal and allowable because they are going through Aces Press to publish the story.

This book is entirely the work of the author who wrote it. While I might have assisted with brain-storming and other ideas about which of my char-acters to use, I didn't have any part in the process or writing or editing the story.

I'm proud and excited that so many authors loved my characters enough that they wanted to write them into their own story. Thank you for supporting them, and me!

READ ON!

Xoxo

Susan Stoker

Thank you Kris. This one's for you.

1

Odessa Hayes slipped off her engagement ring, set it on the counter, and took a long agonizing breath. A life-changing breath. The kind of breath that signified a massive change. A necessary change.

This time, she was done.

No way would she take *him* back.

Grant Mercer was a controlling man who cared about three things and three things only.

Money. Power. Status.

She reached for the open bottle of wine, poured half a glass, and glanced at the time. She should be concerned about the seconds ticking away and what that meant. But she wasn't. Not anymore. What little she had was packed in her suitcases and tucked away in the trunk of her car. She wouldn't make that mistake again.

Although, waiting for him to return home so he could do his best to talk her out of leaving him might not be her brightest idea. But if she didn't, he'd eventually hunt her down. Grant wasn't the kind of man to take no for an answer. To him, the first three nos meant maybe.

At first, she found that trait to be a bit charming, mostly because he wasn't overly aggressive. He was there for her when life had kicked her hard. He showed up when her parents had died. He held her hand through all the tough decisions. He'd even backed off trying to date her during that time. He'd been so sweet it became impossible not to fall in love.

However, it had all been a ruse to rob her of every penny her parents had left her and then steal her dignity.

The moment they settled into a relationship, things changed. It was subtle at first. He'd tell her he didn't want her to worry about a thing. That he and his team would handle everything. When she asked about investing, he'd brush her off or tell her just enough to wet her whistle. He kept her bank account fat enough that she believed her parents' life insurance was protected.

Only, it wasn't.

He stole every fucking penny and she'd been dumb enough to sign on the dotted line.

Then came the blows to her self-esteem. He'd say things like *maybe you should wear the other dress, but it's really up to you. I think you look beautiful in either one.* Then he'd toss in a second comment about how he still preferred one over the other.

Her favorite, though, was when he started in on her hair color and style.

Again, it was nice to have someone who cared, but Grant only cared about how she dressed up his arm. How having a woman who would do what he wanted, when he wanted it, somehow made him more powerful.

But three months ago, she noticed Leslie Anne, the IT manager at one of the dealerships, had subtly changed her hair color and had let it grow. She also changed her flair for fashion and handbags.

Odessa didn't need to be a detective to figure out her fiancé was dipping his dipstick in another woman's oil well.

She climbed onto the stool, lifted the glass, and

sipped slowly. Damn, she would miss this expensive wine. But not enough to stay with Grant. One year was long enough. Too long, if she was being honest, but she didn't dare examine too closely the reasons why she'd chosen to stay.

Only now, she had to face the reality that she was alone—and broke. She'd lost friendships because of Grant and his controlling ways.

Facing them, especially Thane, wasn't going to be easy. Everyone thought she'd been crazy when she'd taken Grant back the last time. No one cared that he wasn't physically abusive; they all agreed he was a shit and that because of him—she'd changed.

But Odessa saw a softer side to Grant. And he did have one. Except he used it to get what he wanted. It was all about manipulation and control and she didn't see it until it was too late.

The roar of an engine filled her ears. Grant loved his sports car. It was one of his most prized possessions. No one was allowed to eat or drink in that damn vehicle. He washed the thing almost every day. She no longer wondered if he cared about his money and material things more than he cared about people. She knew that to be fact. The rumble cut off and deafening silence once again filled the air.

Her heart rattled her chest.

Stay strong.

Squaring her shoulders, she sat up taller. As if that would give her the courage to stand up to the great charismatic Grant Mercer.

The large diamond marquise-cut ring glared at her from the counter. It was a whole carat and it was gorgeous, but it was a bit flashy and pretentious. Sparkly and made a statement. The wrong kind of statement. The ring was more about him and his tastes than what mattered to her. However, Grant couldn't have cared less what she wanted.

All he cared about was impressing others. He showed her off like a trophy he'd pulled off the shelf. As if she was something he'd won. A prize to be coveted and valued. However, not for what she brought to the table. Not for her smarts. Or for even being human. But because he'd fought hard to achieve something, and she was the flashy thing at the end of the rainbow.

And for a while, because of her event planning business, she bought into the idea that he was proud of her and her accomplishments. All the gifts he showered her with made her feel unique and important.

Until they didn't.

The door opened and in strolled Grant. He had this confident swagger that at first she wished she could emulate. Now all it did was annoy her.

"I'm surprised you beat me home." He smiled, meandering into the kitchen like he didn't have a care in the world. He tossed his keys on the counter and set his computer bag on one of the stools. "How was your…" He paused, glancing between her and the ring. "Why aren't you wearing this?" Gently, he lifted it between his thumb and forefinger. "You know how I feel about you taking it off."

"We need to talk," she managed through a thick lump in her throat. She saw no point in dragging this out. Besides, if she didn't do it, she might back out.

"Jesus, not this again." He set the ring back down and pushed it in front of her. "I'm not in the mood to deal with one of your temper tantrums. Put that back on." He ducked his head into the fridge, snagged a beer, and cracked it open. "I can't imagine what set you off this time, but it's getting old."

"Not only am I tired of you telling me what to do, but now you're getting involved in my business. How could you?" Her eyes burned, but she'd be damned if she'd let the tears fall. Her parents had raised her to be a strong, independent woman. Somewhere in the last year, she'd abandoned everything that made up who she was as a person. Her father would be so disappointed.

Grant leaned against the counter and arched a brow. "I have no idea what you're talking about."

"Don't play dumb with me. It's not a good look." She bit down on her lower lip. Pushing Grant's buttons wasn't a good idea in general. He'd never once touched her, but he could be mean. His words cut through her heart like a knife.

"I'm not." He took a big swig of his beer. "Why don't you tell me what you think I did so I can defend myself." He glanced at his watch. "We have to leave for dinner in thirty minutes, so let's make this quick."

"First, I'm not going anywhere with you," she said. "Second, you canceled an event I had accepted last week and committed me to a party for Rufus, of all people. That makes me and my business look bad."

"Seriously? That's what got your panties in a wad?" He chugged his beer. "How many times do we have to have this conversation? You keep taking jobs that are beneath my status in this community." He raised his hand. "If you must continue working after we're married, at least schedule events that make sense. Not stupid little birthday parties for people who have no social standing. That does nothing for you but make you look like a two-bit party planner, not a big-time event coordinator." He pushed from the counter, rinsed out his beer can, and sashayed across the room like he was some kind of diplomat or something. He rested his hand on her shoulder.

It took all the energy she had not to shrug it off. "Oh, and Rufus is high society?" She swallowed her breath. She never understood Rufus' and Grant's relationship. The only thing they had in common was they were both born into money. But Rufus had been a rebel without a cause in high school. Their only connection back then had been football and drugs.

After they graduated, Rufus joined the military. When he came back, he opened a private security firm. That firm handled all security for every dealership Grant owned.

"He's a businessman in this community. People respect him." Grant squeezed a little too tightly. "You're about to be my wife. I have a reputation to maintain and standards. You need to live up to those. Rufus has important contacts—government contacts—and that means I could sell a fleet of cars to them. That's a big deal. If you insist on having a career—which isn't necessary at all—then you need to consider what's best for our future." He dared to kiss her cheek. "But when the time comes for us to have children, you will give it up. Now, I'm going to go take a shower. I expect you to be ready when I get out." He headed toward the hallway but turned at the base of the stairs. "Oh, and wear that cute little red number I like. I'll lay it out on the bed for you." He waved his hand over his head. "Put your hair up. It's more sophisticated that way. This dinner is important, so try not to ramble too much and do not swear. I hope you've been reading those books I gave you. We really need to work on your knowledge and vocabulary." And with that statement, he disappeared up the stairs.

She didn't bother confronting him about Leslie Anne. What would have been the point? He would have denied that too. He would have called her paranoid.

Just like he had when she asked him about her money.

How could she have been so blind? Had she

been that desperate for love after her parents died that she hadn't seen any of the signs until it was too late? God, how she missed her folks. They had been her biggest supporters. Her champions. They loved her without question. Never judged her life choices, not even when she decided to leave college after her second year and travel. They understood how heartbroken she'd been when she and Thane had broken up.

Thane had been her world. Her everything. They had made so many plans for their future, but she hadn't anticipated how hard military life would be. She tried. She had given it her all.

But it wasn't enough.

And she wasn't about to ask Thane to give up his dreams. He thrived in the Marines. It had become his calling. Twice they tried to get back together, but she could never bring herself to move. Fallport was her home. It's where she wanted to spend her life. Thane's original contract with the Marines had been for six years. That wasn't forever.

But she couldn't ask him to turn his back on something that gave him purpose. That would have been selfish and he would have ended up resenting it. Just like if she had followed him, she would have loathed their life together.

Then he got married and broke her heart.

After her parents passed, Grant came in like a knight in shining armor. He gave her a shoulder to cry on. At the time, his controlling ways felt more like love and devotion. As if all he wanted was for her to be happy and he knew exactly what she needed.

Looking back, she could see clearly how he stripped her of all her power and she was now left with nothing but a few thousand dollars in the bank and a car, which he'd technically bought for her, but at least it was in her name.

And that was it because two months ago he'd sold her family home and everything in it. Sure, she'd signed off on the sale and moved in with him. However, deep down she knew she was making a mistake.

Everyone knew.

Including Thane, and he'd even told her so. One of the few times he hadn't been nice about it since his return to Fallport, Virginia.

Seeing Thane again had been a gut punch. She knew he'd gotten divorced, but they had stopped communicating when he married.

Gripping the door, she stepped out into the warm summer evening air. She'd been dating

Grant for about three months when Thane had returned after leaving the Marines. Grant made it quite clear she was to stay as far away from Thane as possible.

Thane was not only her past, but he was a man whom she'd once had a relationship with and Grant didn't like it when people gossiped—about her. If she even looked at Thane, Grant would get upset.

Always a double standard.

She scurried toward her vehicle, climbed behind the steering wheel, and texted Sylvia and Chrissy.

They were the only friends she had left, though both relationships were strained. But they both told her if she ever left Grant, they would be there to help her pick up the pieces.

Odessa: *I did it. I gave the ring back. And I left. I mean left, left. Packed my bags and now I'm homeless. LOL. I've got a hotel room for tonight while I figure things out. I'm heading to On The Rocks. I haven't been there in almost a year. Anyone care to join me?*

Chrissy: *I'm stuck at the ER for the next hour. How about you pick up takeout? We can meet back at my place. I've got the whole weekend off!*

The first tear fell. At least she hadn't totally burned that bridge. The last time she'd spoken to Chrissy, they'd fought. Hard.

Sylvia: *Let's meet at my house. I'll be home in thirty and cancel the hotel. You're staying with me.*

The tears flowed freely.

Odessa: *I would love that. One thing, though, and it's not what you think. I don't want a big pity party. I don't want the gossip. So, please don't tell the world I dumped Grant. Everyone will know soon enough.*

Sylvia: *At least you're saying YOU dumped that jerk. And I get it. Gossip in this town sucks. How about we go camping this weekend? It will be like old times.*

Chrissy: *Grant's going to deny it anyway, so no reason to even talk about it. And camping sounds amazing. I could use a little girls' trip. See you bitches soon!*

Odessa pressed the start button and without looking back, she pulled away from the big house on the corner lot with the massive pool in the backyard. She didn't need Grant or his money. What she needed was to find her old self and rebuild her life in a way that would make her parents proud.

Thane Bishop didn't go out to dinner very often, much to his mother's dismay. She constantly tried to get him to have a more active social life. Both with his buddies and with the ladies.

Specifically when it came to Odessa.

His mom meant well, but she didn't seem to understand that the moment Odessa accepted that damn fucking engagement ring, Thane was totally out of the running.

Not that he was ever in the running.

Just because she'd broken up with Grant once didn't mean she'd do it again. Besides, what Thane and Odessa had was a long time ago. Hell, they were barely friends now, and she'd made it clear that she didn't want him in her life.

Thane pulled open the door to On The Rocks and glanced around. The nice thing about Zeke's place was that Grant Mercer wouldn't be caught dead in it. He believed a place like On The Rocks was beneath him. Everything was beneath Grant. The man was an arrogant prick and Thane couldn't understand what Odessa saw in him. She wasn't a flashy girl. At least not when they had been together. But a lot had changed over the years.

"Hey, man." Zeke Calhoun, the bar owner, waved from behind the counter. "It's good to see you out… socially."

Thane chuckled. He was used to the razzing. He'd grown up on it, having been more of an introvert. "Every once in a while, I suffer through dealing with people." He shook Zeke's hand.

"The gang's at the table in the back corner," Zeke said. "They have a few pitchers of beer, but I know how much you like an espresso martini. Can I bring you one?"

"I'd absolutely love one, thanks." Thane nodded. Zeke hadn't been a part of the community when he'd left for the Marines. But Zeke certainly had been a welcome addition. As well as some of the new search and rescue crew members. All of them were worth getting out of his shell more often.

"It won't take but a couple of minutes," Zeke said. "Tell the guys I'll bring some apps as well."

"You're the best." He zigzagged through the Thursday night crowd to the far corner. Sitting in the booth was his old friend Blaze. They had first met back in the Marines. Next to Blaze was Weston, who married Haven, a local girl Thane had known most of his life. Across from Weston were his two cousins, Ethan and Rocky.

Now those two were quite interesting. Polar opposites in many ways, but they were great men. The kind of men you wanted at your six when going into battle.

"You made it," Weston said. "Thought maybe you were going to stand us up."

"My mother would have chased me out of the house if I tried to cancel," Thane admitted. "Sometimes I think she's tired of having me around."

"How is your mom?" Ethan asked. "Is she feeling any better?"

"She has good and bad days." Thane eased into the booth. The first six months after his dad passed away, his mom struggled to function emotionally. But it was her autoimmune disorder that now reared its ugly head. She'd been dealing with multiple sclerosis for years, but lately it had been causing her some real problems. "Where's Chuck and Jett?"

"Chuck had some things going on with the kids and Jett's on baby duty tonight," Blaze said. "Talon and Lincoln still might join us, but it's up in the air."

One of the waitresses appeared carrying a tray of appetizers and Thane's drink.

"How can you drink those things?" Weston said. "Besides the fact I'd be up all night, you look like a moron."

Thane laughed. He raised his glass, making sure

he stuck out his pinky before bringing it to his lips. "Hmmmm, that's delish."

"You're such a girl." Rocky shook his head.

"Don't let my wife hear you talk like that," Weston said with an arched brow.

Thane leaned back, shifting his gaze. He promised his mom he'd at least check out the possible single girls. He spotted two. Unfortunately, he'd known them back in the day. One was recently divorced and he knew the reason why.

He didn't want to deal with that baggage.

The other lady was also divorced with two small children.

Nope. He wasn't interested in being a stepfather. If that made him an asshole, then he'd gladly wear that badge. It wasn't that he didn't like children, because he did. He loved them. At one time, he thought he wanted a couple of his own. But his life didn't turn out that way.

Besides, between his father's death and his mother's health problems, he didn't have time to date.

There. He checked out a few of the singles. He'd kept his promise and he wouldn't be lying to his mama.

"Don't look now, but Odessa just walked through the front door," Rocky said.

Thane's heart jumped to his throat at the mere mention of her name. He resented that she had that effect. Resented that one week with her had stirred up all those damn love feelings he had for her that he believed he'd put to rest years ago. He shouldn't care so deeply. What they had ended when she couldn't commit and fell in love with someone else. It didn't matter that his marriage failed; he'd accepted that he and Odessa were over.

Until she'd shown up at his doorstep the first time she and Grant had broken up. That lasted all of a week.

But it was just long enough to fuck with Thane's head.

He glanced over his shoulder. There she stood, in the center of the bar, clutching her purse. Her eyes were big, and they shifted left and right, as if she were searching for someone.

Anyone.

"What the hell is she doing here?" Thane muttered. "This is not the kind of place she and Grant hang out." His gaze zoned in on her left hand.

No ring.

That didn't mean shit.

He'd been married for four years and his ex-wife used to take hers off to have it cleaned all the time.

The real question he should be asking himself was why the fuck did he bother looking?

Or why was he pushing himself to a standing position to meet her in the middle of the bar?

Perhaps it was the confused and sad look etched in her beautiful teal-blue eyes. He'd seen that look before. If he was being honest, it had been there since her parents had died.

He certainly could understand that. There was a big hole in his heart since his father passed and watching his mother grapple with grief and her health broke his soul.

"Where are you going?" Weston grabbed his wrist. "I'm sure her fiancé will be following her in shortly and the last thing we all want to do is watch you get into a brawl and have me arrest you because you and Grant can't be civil with one another."

"I second that and Grant is always two steps behind," Blaze agreed.

"Only, he wouldn't dare step foot in this place."

Ethan raised his beer. "He thinks anyone who frequents this bar is low-hanging fruit."

"All the more reason for me to go find out if she's okay." Thane took one more hit of his drink and left his buddies in the dust. Mostly because he didn't want to hear how Odessa wasn't his problem.

He already knew that.

But one couldn't erase over twenty years of history.

By the time he approached her, she'd perched herself at the bar. "Hey, Odessa," he said. "You look a little lost."

She snorted, her go-to chuckle when she was anything but good. "Not lost, just early."

"Meeting Grant?"

She burst out laughing. But she obviously didn't find it funny since her eyes watered. Clearing her throat, she turned her head and wiped her perfectly manicured finger across her cheek. "No. It's a girls' night and I'm waiting for our take-out order."

"Are you okay?" He hoisted himself up on the stool and squeezed her thigh. Touching her was a bold move. It was possessive—and she didn't belong to him. Not now and most likely never. A fact his mind had accepted, but his heart struggled to understand the cruelty of being teased with a small taste of what life could be like with the one he'd let slip through his fingers.

"I'm fine." She narrowed her stare. "Why wouldn't I be?"

He reached for her hand, holding it up, and arched his brow.

She jerked her arm.

"What happened this time?" he asked with a sigh. He shouldn't care. Odessa had told him months ago that she loved Grant. That he was the perfect man for her and that she was happy.

Thane didn't believe a word she had said. However, he had to respect her wishes.

Unless Grant broke her heart.

Or worse, because Grant was an asshole.

Her lower lip quivered. She tried so hard to be strong and independent. He loved that about her, but Grant chiseled away at her core personality. She couldn't see it—or wouldn't. However, everyone else could.

"Come on, Odessa. Talk to me."

"There's nothing to discuss."

"Seriously? You're on the verge of tears." He took her hand and kissed the inside of the palm. "Did he hurt you?" Thane held his breath while his heart thumped in his chest like a jackhammer struggling to cut through concrete.

"Why do you always go there?" She cocked her head. "He's not abusive."

"Maybe not with his hands, but he doesn't treat you well and you can do better."

"Better?" She lowered her chin. "Are we going to have that discussion again?"

"I didn't mean me."

"Honestly, it doesn't matter if you meant you or any other man in this town. I don't need the judgment and frankly, I'm tired of it. Grant isn't a bad man. Misguided at times, but my personal life isn't on the cutting board for everyone to chop up and spit out."

"All I want is for you to be happy and since I've come back to Fallport, I haven't seen that." He leaned back, wishing he'd brought his beverage. He could use some alcohol right about now.

"Let me ask you this." She lowered her chin. "Are you happy?"

"I'm not unhappy and we're not talking about me. For the record, this isn't me judging you. However, Grant doesn't respect you. He makes demands of you. He expects you—"

"Stop," she said. "My love life is none of your business anymore."

"Why are you being so combative with me?" he asked. "I'm trying to help."

"No. You're trying to get me to admit shit about Grant. You want me to tell you I have problems in my relationship."

He knew there were issues, so he didn't need her to tell him anything. He did want to be a good friend. A sounding board. But he had no idea how to cross over into that space where she could trust him again. It didn't help that he'd made a massive mistake a few months ago by filling her in on the fact that he had feelings. No, it was worse than that. He used the word love. What a fucking idiot.

He should have kept that to himself.

The hostess came over, set a couple of bags on the counter, and thanked her for her order.

"I've gotta run," she said.

He curled his fingers around her wrist. "I'm always around if you ever need someone to talk to." He raised his hands. "I promise. No judgments. I mean it when I say I only want you to be happy. That includes if it means being with Grant." Lifting her hand to his mouth, he pressed his lips against her ring finger, letting them linger, holding her gaze.

A tear escaped her eye.

Damn it. He hated being right, even about that asshole.

"Call me day or night," he said. "I will always be there for you."

"So you keep telling me." She climbed down from the barstool, turned, and disappeared.

Thane raked his fingers through his hair. He had no idea how to reach her, much less help her. Of course, he had no idea what the problem was this time, but the rumor mill in this town would sure be discussing it soon enough. He let out a long breath. Gossip was the last thing she needed.

"Everything okay with her?" Zeke appeared at his side with an arched brow and a strong hand on his shoulder.

"Honestly, I don't believe so."

"That's the first time I've seen her in here in months," Zeke said. "She used to come in every ladies' night with her friends. But once she started dating Grant, that all changed. Maybe she finally saw the light."

"She wasn't wearing her ring, but my ex-wife didn't always wear hers and I never wore a wedding band."

Zeke cocked his head. "Why not?"

"I tried. Trust me. But when Tonia told me to stop making myself miserable with the damn thing, I smiled like a kid in a candy store." Thane laughed. "She and I had our fair share of troubles. Jealousy wasn't one of them. At least on her part."

"Why did you get divorced?" Zeke asked. "If you don't mind me asking, because all you've ever said was it didn't work out, and Blaze said it had nothing to do with cheating."

"It didn't. Except Tonia wanted us to bring another woman into our bed. I wasn't interested."

Zeke's eyes grew as wide as the ocean. He banged his chest and coughed. "We all joke about having a threesome, but your ex seriously wanted to?"

Thane nodded. "I knew she'd had a couple of things with girls before we got together. Never bothered me. I just never thought she'd want us to have a relationship with the dog groomer."

"Hey, at least it wasn't a dude."

"Oh, Tonia would have been down for that too," Thane said. "Last I spoke to her, she and her boyfriend were into swinging."

"This might get me sucker punched, but how did you not know this about her? You were married for four years, right?"

These kinds of questions used to drive Thane nuts. Not because it made him feel like a fool, because he didn't. He and Tonia had a great relationship. Sure, they fought like any other couple, but truth be told, the only time they struggled was when they split. "Tonia's a bit younger than I am. She didn't know what she wanted when we got married. She did what she thought she was supposed to do when she fell in love. As she grew into herself, she realized monogamy wasn't for her, but she said she loved me and didn't want to lose me." Thane shook his head. "There was no way I could live my life the way she wanted me to and for the next year, we began to struggle for the first time since we'd been together. We both decided it was best to end the marriage. It was honestly a rough go of it for both of us because we did—and in some ways still—love each other."

"You're still friends?"

"I consider her a good friend." Thane nodded. "She's a good person. I wish her well. I don't agree with her lifestyle choices, but as long as she's happy, I don't judge."

Zeke pointed toward the front door. "You kind of judge Odessa."

"Because she's not happy and she's with a prick

who treats her like a possession, not a person." Thane rubbed the back of his neck. "At least I know with Tonia, she's picking and choosing people who want to be in the same world as she is. There's a lot of respect and trust that comes with that kind of lifestyle. And while Tonia was young when she and I married, that girl knows how to stand up for herself." Thane glanced over his shoulder. "Somewhere along the way, Odessa has forgotten how to use her voice. About the only time she does is when she wants to tell me to fuck off."

"Is that what she did tonight?"

"Not really. But I hit a nerve," Thane said. "I just hope she can break free from this insane hold Grant has over her." He held up his hand. "I'm not saying that because I've got a thing for her. That was over a long time ago."

"You still care for her."

"Of course I do. I've known her since we were in diapers. But I'm not hung up on her, like all you idiots and my mom seem to think I am. I'm just tired of watching her become a shell of a person. I blame that on Grant."

"We all do." Zeke nodded. "I've got to get back to work and those yahoos are giving you the evil eye."

Thane laughed. "Yeah, they didn't want me to come over and play knight in shining armor."

"You do act a little obsessed sometimes." Zeke slapped him on the back. "I get it. I do. But she's really not your problem and while we can all agree Grant's a selfish egomaniac, he's never done anything criminal or lifted a hand to her."

Thane couldn't argue that point. However, abuse came in many shapes and forms and Grant had found a way to control Odessa. To break her personality down and that broke Thane's heart.

2

Thane had a death grip on his thermos. He followed the trail toward the lower ridge campsites. His heart pulsed in his chest like a wild rabbit. He and Odessa used to hike these trails back in high school. They—and all their friends—would pack their camping gear and spend weekends during the summer camping, fishing, and doing their best not to get into trouble so they could do it all again the following weekend. These trails—the campsites—were Thane's happy place. It was, in part, why he chose park ranger over other job opportunities when he returned to Fallport.

A crime scene with a search and rescue was not a good way to start his day.

"Ethan texted." Chuck strolled along at Thane's

side. "He's sending Lincoln, Tal, Brayden, and Rocky to start the search." Chuck was a few years older. However, Thane had known him and his wife Renee his entire life. They were more like family than friends. "I've told Jett and Andy to work with them. Cooper will join in the search efforts once we get to the site."

"Who found the bodies?" Thane tried to swallow. However, that was a struggle. Not only was his throat dry, but his pulse throbbed right in the center of it. It was like a frog jumped in his mouth and couldn't decide if it wanted to head south or come back out the same way it got in.

"A young couple went for an early morning hike over at the lower pass. When they looked down to take some pictures, they spotted them."

"But no sign of Odessa?" Thane choked on her name. Normally, it rolled off his tongue like warm butter.

"Not at the campsite or where her friends were found," Chuck said. "I'm the one who booked the site for them." Chuck took the right fork in the path toward the lower pass. "They had the campsite until Sunday."

"How'd she seem to you?"

"Honestly?" Chuck shrugged. "She was a

bundle of nerves. She kept looking at her phone, which was constantly buzzing in her hands. Chrissy kept telling her to relax and to turn the damn thing off."

"I think something happened between her and Grant."

"Are you going to start tossing out accusations?" Chuck paused right before the clearing. "Because that wouldn't be a good idea. I know how you feel about that man. Hell, none of us really like him, but that doesn't mean he had anything to do with this."

"Seriously? Two girls are dead, and Odessa is missing." Thane planted his hands on his hips. "She came into On The Rocks Thursday night. She hasn't been in that bar since she started dating that prick. She wasn't wearing her engagement ring. She seemed off."

"That doesn't mean jack shit and you know it."

"Didn't you say someone complained about the girls fighting last night?"

Chuck nodded. "Another group mentioned this morning that they heard the girls having a disagreement at about midnight. It got heated, and they were about to tell them to shut up when it got quiet."

"Could they hear what they were arguing about?" Thane asked.

"Nope," Chuck said, jerking his thumb over his shoulder. "I need to know you're not going to go spout off conspiracy theories. Let Weston and Haven do their jobs." He cocked his head. "They are good cops and will figure out whoever killed those girls." Chuck rested his hand on Thane's shoulder. "And we'll find Odessa."

Thane sucked in a deep breath, letting it out in a huff through his nose. Two girls dead. Murdered. One missing. He knew the odds. If this were a random killing, well, Odessa's chances of being alive were slim.

If it was Grant?

Her days were numbered, if he hadn't already done the deed.

But Thane wasn't a cop. What did he know?

He'd been a Marine Raider. A sniper. When he wasn't sitting overwatch, he specialized in unconventional warfare and special reconnaissance. He trained friendly foreign governments. He went behind enemy lines. He assessed the situation, reported back, and then did what he'd been trained to do.

It wasn't pretty.

It was dangerous and often left carnage behind.

But he was fucking good at it—especially the shooting part.

However, leaving had been a no-brainer the day his mother called to tell him his father died. Being a park ranger was supposed to be a nice quiet job where not much happened.

He'd returned last year right after bones were found on the side of the trails, digging up all of Winslet's family drama. He was kind of glad he'd missed that one. He'd known Winslet back in the day and while he felt bad for what she'd gone through, she came out the other side better than ever.

She and Jett were now married and had a little kid.

Life sure took strange turns.

"You're not saying anything and that makes me nervous." Chuck arched a brow.

"I can't promise I won't interject my thoughts." Thane raised his hand. "However, any opinion I give will be based in fact, not emotion."

"I can live with that." Chuck waved his finger. "Just remember you represent Parks and Recreation."

"Noted." Thane continued on the path, doing

his best to push his personal feelings to the side. It wasn't easy, but Chuck was right. He had a job to do and it didn't involve solving the crime. He'd look over both crime scenes. He needed to see for himself the state of the campsite. To see if there were any clues left behind. To chat with law enforcement and gauge their thoughts. If they would tell him anything. Then join the rest of the search and rescue in the hunt for Odessa.

As soon as they reached the clearing, he made a beeline for Haven. "What can you tell me? And don't give me the standard bullshit."

"I wasn't planning on it," Haven said. "They were wearing their pajamas and were barefoot. The bathrooms are in the opposite direction, but it's possible they could have gotten turned around." She stood near the crime scene tape. The medical examiner had already covered the bodies. The CSI unit was still gathering evidence and taking pictures. She widened her stance, looping her fingers into her belt.

Sometimes it was hard to believe that Haven had become a cop. While she was a few years older than Thane, they had been friendly growing up. Her strict upbringing had made it difficult for her to chase her dreams. Not that he ever knew what they were, but her parents had a choke hold over her choices.

That was until she left for college.

"You don't sound very convincing," he said.

She pointed to the cliff above. "It appears they fell from up there, but we don't know that for sure. The ME needs to do an autopsy. There's also a trail of blood from the campsite to the drop-off."

"It's not that big of a drop." He glanced up. "Less than a flight of stairs. I'd argue that one could have survived that fall."

"I'd have to agree with that statement depending on how they landed," she said. "But that trail of blood also indicates at least one of them was dragged, so they could have been dead before falling and someone pushed them over." Haven raised her hand. "This is all speculation and I'm only telling you because we're both friends with the one who's still missing."

"Are there any wounds on the body that indicate foul play?"

"There is some bruising, but we didn't see anything like a possible gunshot or a stabbing, if that's what you're getting at."

"Any sign of what happened to Odessa?"

Haven shook her head. "Weston is over at the

campsite. He might know something that I don't." She glanced at her watch. "We were going to meet up in about ten minutes to go over everything."

"I'm going to take a walk over there now. Anything you want me to tell him?"

"Nope." Haven curled her fingers around Thane's forearm. "You should know that we called Grant."

"Why the hell would you do that?" Thane clenched his fists. Grant was the last person they needed up on these trails.

"He's her fiancé." Haven cocked her head and pursed her lips. "She has no one else in this town. We needed to notify someone that she's missing. Right now, she's a big missing piece of this puzzle."

Thane supposed that made sense, though he wished they had waited. "Is he on his way?"

"We told him that right now the trails are closed to the public but if he wanted to help in the search, he could report to the parking lot. Ethan and his team will be organizing the volunteers there."

"Anything else I should know?"

"Nothing at this time," Haven said, lowering her gaze.

"What aren't you telling me?"

Haven glanced over her shoulder. "Not here.

Call Weston and me later tonight or stop by and we'll talk. Okay?"

"Got it. Thanks." Thane considered himself a patient man. That philosophy was being tested. He scanned the area, taking mental notes of everything. He did his best to categorize what he saw.

Accidents happened all the time on these trails. People went missing, especially after dark or if they went hiking in the afternoon and miscalculated the sunset. Every so often, someone died. Usually, it was an accident.

But two women falling off a small cliff?

Something felt off.

Especially when Odessa was missing, which didn't look good for her. Thane understood that made her a person of interest, even if Haven didn't come out and say it.

Carefully, he made his way back to the trail and headed up toward the camping grounds which took about six minutes. The terrain wasn't overly difficult, but it wouldn't be easy to navigate at night.

"Hey, Thane," Weston said as he approached.

Thane pointed to the tent. "Find anything of interest in there?"

"Some blood stains." Weston folded his arms across his chest. "And there was a trail of blood that leads to the lower ridge. The CSI unit has taken a bunch of samples. We should know later today or tomorrow what samples belong to the victims and if we have a third person's sample. Or even a fourth."

"You think there might be more?"

"I don't know," Weston said. "But I don't believe those two girls wandered off and fell." He arched a brow. "That leaves me with two possible scenarios. The first is that Odessa had something to do with it."

"Come on. We both know that's not possible."

"I'm a cop. I've seen some shit. Like last year when we all found out that Winslet's father had killed his parents. So, anything's possible," Weston said. "Whether you like it or not, it's an angle I have to consider and investigate, and I have to do it with an open mind."

Thane rolled his neck. He understood Weston had a job to do. But he didn't like it one fucking bit. He nodded. "I take it the second option is someone else killed Sylvia and Chrissy and then kidnapped Odessa."

"That's one working theory."

"You have more?"

"We have to consider the possibility that if we're

dealing with a killer, he could have dumped her body somewhere else."

"I don't like that option. What's behind door number three?"

Weston waved his arm. "That she's out there, hiding somewhere, until she feels safe to come out."

"I think I'll hold on to that one," Thane mumbled. His stomach churned the bitter coffee he'd been sipping all morning. Suddenly, he wished he hadn't had that second cup. "What else can you tell me?"

"Nothing right now, but we'll talk tonight."

"That's what your wife said."

"Yeah, she texted me. She figured you might try to pump me for information." Weston let out a long breath. "Look. I know you're worried. I understand you and Odessa have a long history and you care about her. But right now, I need you to work with the search and rescue team and let me and my wife do our jobs. We're kind of good at it."

"I know. And I appreciate everything you're doing." Thane glanced over his shoulder. "I need to ask you one more question."

"Okay."

"You called Grant. What was his demeanor like when you told him? What did he say?"

"To be honest, it was a mixed bag." Weston took Thane by the biceps and guided him farther away from the campsite and away from those working the crime scene. "At first, he acted like one might expect. Shock. Fear. He asked what I would consider normal questions."

"Like what?"

"He wanted to know who saw the girls last. What time they checked in at the site. Things like that."

"So, he knew she'd gone camping." Thane lifted his cap and scratched the back of his head. "If they were still together, I'm shocked he'd let go on a girls' trip."

"We need to table this conversation for later," Weston said softly. "I need to get back to this investigation, but I'll call when I get a break. Or Haven will."

"All right. I appreciate it." Thane adjusted his cap. "I'm going to radio search and rescue and start looking. I'll be in touch."

"Let me know if you find anything."

"Will do." Thane wouldn't stop until he found Odessa. She had to be okay. He'd never forgive himself if anything bad had happened to her.

Thane glanced at his watch. It had been three hours since they'd begun the search for Odessa. He lifted his water bottle and took a hearty swig. Leaning against a tree, he scanned the area. He and Tal had zigzagged off one of the main trails near the campsite. They bushwhacked through some thick brush until they came to a clearing.

He pulled out his cell and checked for messages.

Nothing.

Of course, if anyone had found her, they would have radioed, but they had no idea if Odessa had her cell or not. Haven mentioned the IT team was working on pinging the phone's location, but no one had brought that intel to his attention.

However, he did have a notification for a press release given by fucking Grant.

"Jesus," Thane muttered.

"What is it?" Tal asked from a fallen tree he'd perched himself on. Tal had come to search and rescue by way of the UK Special Boat Service. Oddly, he was a barber and a damn good one.

"Grant gave a statement of some kind." Thane tapped on the link. "Fuck. He spoke to reporters. Live."

"You've got to be kidding me? Before or after the cops spoke to the press?" Tal strolled across the clearing and peered over his shoulder.

"That, I don't know." It took a couple of seconds for the video to load since the cell reception wasn't all that great.

"Odessa," Grant started. "I know you're scared. Whatever happened, I'm sure… well, I'm sure it had to be an accident. Please, just come home, and we will work through it. Everyone is so worried about you. But we can't help you unless you come back. If anyone has seen Odessa, I beg you to help her and bring her home. Thank you."

"What the fuck," Thane mumbled. "Did I hear that right?" He glanced between the cell and over his shoulder.

"It sounds like Grant believes she may know something about what happened—"

"Or had something to do with it." Thane swallowed. Hard.

"Grant is implying she's hiding because of what happened." Tal stepped back into the clearing. "I can see anyone in that position asking for her to come home, but if that were me, and it was my wife, I'd be begging whoever possibly had her to let her go. I'd be asking everyone who might have seen her to come forward with any possible information.

I'd also probably offer a ransom, especially if I had his kind of money."

"But he didn't do any of those things," Thane said. "If anything, he made it sound like she did something wrong."

"You mentioned she was upset Thursday but didn't actually say she and Grant called it quits."

"No, she didn't. But the fact she went camping with Sylvia and Chrissy tells me she did."

"Why?"

"Because those two hated Grant and believed the relationship was bad for Odessa. They were more vocal about it than I was. So much so that it nearly ruined their friendship." Thane tucked his cell in his back pocket. He'd deal with his million and one questions about it with Weston and Haven later. "Sylvia mentioned to me once that Grant told Odessa he didn't like her hanging out with them. That he suggested to Odessa if she couldn't surround herself with people who supported them, then he would have to reconsider their living arrangement. I can understand not wanting to have people around who don't support you. But this went beyond surrounding yourself with friends and family who actually care and don't have some ulterior motive. Grant would speak for Odessa,"

Thane said. "I've seen that firsthand and it's gross."

"I've seen that too." Tal nodded. "I was out with my family and ran into Grant and Odessa. He's not a friendly man, but we knew Odessa before she started dating him, so we said hello. He was on her like flies on shit. Wrapped his arm around her waist and pulled her so close it couldn't be called romantic. More like a death grip. We were just trying to be neighborly. Every time we asked a question, he answered, and then before we knew it, they were sitting at their table, ignoring us."

"Sounds about right," Thane said. "When I first returned to Fallport, Odessa seemed genuinely happy to see me. I'd lost my dad a few months before and her parents had recently died. We bonded over that. But Grant didn't like her hanging around her high school sweetheart."

"I can kind of understand how he might be jealous." Tal arched a brow. "I'm a secure man, but I might have a problem with my wife going to breakfast with her ex-boyfriend on a regular basis."

"If that were the case, yeah, I get it." Thane chuckled. "However, I wasn't a threat."

"But you still carry a torch."

"Not even the point," Thane said. "The few times Odessa and I met for coffee, all we did was talk about her folks, my dad, or how my mom was getting along. It was never about our past. I didn't see her that way. Not during that time. Grant's the one who made it ugly. He gave her an ultimatum and she told me for the sake of her relationship, she couldn't spend time with me anymore. Honestly, I understood. I knew Grant back in the day. We didn't like each other then, and not much has changed. But if she even smiled at me when we passed on the street, he would get in my face about it."

"How did he treat her when the three of you were in the same space? Say like at a party. Or if you were in the same restaurant?"

"Mostly, he treated her like the little woman—or a small child, which pissed me off even more. It was as if she wasn't capable of taking care of herself. It went beyond being a gentleman and opening doors and shit like that. It was downright controlling. Condescending."

"Crazy question here." Tal cocked his head. "If she finally dumped his ass and was back hanging with her besties, why the hell wouldn't she tell you?"

"I'm guessing it might have to do with the last time she broke up with Grant."

"You mean because she went from his bed to yours?" Tal asked.

"No. It wasn't that so much." Thane shook his head. "I told her she could do better than Grant and that I might be that man."

"Shit. Seriously? Right after she broke up with him?"

Thane nodded. "It gets worse."

"Christ. What did you do?"

"I might have told I still loved her."

"Damn," Tal said. "What did she say?"

Thane rubbed the side of his cheek. This wasn't an easy conversation to have with anyone. "There was swearing. Lots of *how fucking dare you do this to me.* Then she grabbed me by the shirt and stared at me like she wanted to murder me. I took a step back, and she kissed me so hard we tumbled back on the sofa. It led to a full-on make-out session that might have landed us in bed had my mother not interrupted us." The joys of being a grown man living in a garage apartment above his mama's house. "Odessa got up, walked out the door, and went back to Grant the next day. They were engaged like a month later."

"Shit. I'm sorry. But this is better than those reality TV shows my wife likes."

"You're an asshole," Thane muttered, though he welcomed the comic relief.

"I've been told that once or twice."

"Anyway. Reality sunk in and Odessa told me that she made a mistake. That she was hurting and that any man's bed would have done the trick."

"Ouch."

"Yeah, well, I did feel like I was taking advantage, so it was easy to back off," Thane said. "But I figured she just needed some time. I can be a patient man. Only, she had that ring on her finger and she changed pretty quickly. I told Odessa that I would always be there for her as a friend. That she mattered to me and that I would never do anything to hurt her or her relationship with Grant."

"Does he know what happened between the two of you?"

"I doubt it because if he did, I'm sure he'd have something to say to me about it and I doubt he would have taken her back. However, he's made it clear once or twice that I'm to stay as far away from Odessa as possible and she's been towing that line."

Snap.

Crack.

Snap.

Tal raised his hand and spun on his heel.

Thane craned his neck toward the noise. His military training kicked into high gear. He'd spent much of his career on a hilltop—alone—with his eye stuck to a scope. His job was to scan the area. To watch for danger. To be the eye in the sky, so to speak. But his ears had to be as sharp as his eyes. He had to listen for shifts in the wind. Not just because it could affect the trajectory of his bullet but because it could mean approaching disaster from above.

Snap.

Snap.

Sniffle.

"That's not an animal," he whispered, easing out of the clearing toward a grouping of bushes.

A few branches waved in the windless air.

Resting his hand on the butt of his weapon, he pulled back some of the bush.

A dirty, bruised, and blood-covered Odessa bolted from behind her hiding place. She leaped over a log, nearly falling flat on her face. She pushed to a standing position and took off running, arms flapping wildly at her sides.

"Odessa," he called, chasing after her. It took all of thirty seconds for him to catch up. He curled his arm around her waist, hoisting her bare feet off the ground.

"Let me go!" She kicked her legs. Shook her head. Thrashed her arms. All in an attempt to break free. "Leave me alone!"

"It's me, Odessa. I'm not going to hurt you."

"I don't know any Odessa. And I don't know you." She hurled her foot into his kneecap.

He flinched but kept his grip on her tiny body. Her shirt was torn and covered in blood. She had a massive bump on the side of her head as well as cuts on her legs and arms.

God only knew what had happened. What she saw. Who she saw.

"Odessa, I need you to calm down," he whispered against her ear. "You're safe. It's me, Thane."

"I don't know any Thane." She continued to fight, jerking her head back and smacking his nose.

He winced. His eyes watered. "Shit, that hurt," he mumbled, holding her tighter. "Why are you fighting me? I'm here to help you."

"I radioed Haven," Tal said in a calm, almost singsong voice. "She's called for a medic."

"Good." Thane leaned against a tree, both arms wrapped tightly around Odessa, who wouldn't stop wiggling. She lowered her head and her teeth dug into his skin.

"Jesus, stop that," he managed behind a tight jaw. "I don't want to have to hurt you."

"Let. Me. Go." She continued to oscillate, her legs and arms nailing him left and right like a toddler having a temper tantrum.

"I will set you down if you promise to stop fighting and let me help you," he said about as calmly as he could.

Her body went limp.

"Odessa, do not run," he said. "I need to look at your injuries."

"I don't know you and I don't want your help."

"She could have a concussion and be dazed and confused," Tal said softly. "We might want to try a different tactic."

"I'm going to set you down." Thane eased her to the clearing. "You really don't know who I am? Or who that is?" He pointed to Tal.

"Should I?" she asked with a quivering lower lip. Her eyes were as big as a deer's caught in headlights.

"We're both park rangers. You and I grew up

together and Tal over there moved to town a few years ago. You know his wife."

"I don't think so," she mumbled, fingering the badge on his shirt.

"What's your name?" He knelt before her and examined the bump more closely. There was a deep cut that needed stitches and another large bump on the base of her head. Dried blood clung to her skin like warpaint. Whatever happened, she needed medical attention. Tal was right. He needed to treat this as if he'd found a stranger lost in the woods.

She blinked, staring at him with tears in her big beautiful eyes. "I don't know."

"Do you know what day it is?" Thane had known Odessa his entire life. She was a shitty liar. She once tried to fake being sick so she could avoid taking her biology exam. Her parents didn't believe her. Not for one second.

She shook her head, groaning and blinking out a few tears.

Tal tapped his shoulder. "I'm going to mark our location so Haven and the medics can find us off the path."

Thane nodded, keeping his focus on Odessa. "Do you have any idea how you got here?"

"No," she whispered.

"Okay. Can you tell me the last thing you remember?" He'd seen a few buddies deal with PTSD and memory loss after being tortured. Or shot and nearly dying. He understood putting too much pressure on her wouldn't be helpful, but he had to go through the motions. He had to ask some questions.

He had to try.

"I don't know. I don't know." She stared at him with wide, terrified eyes. He'd seen many different looks and faces on Odessa, including fear. But this? This he'd never seen before.

"Did you hear me and my buddy talking?" he asked.

"Some of it," she said. "My ears are ringing. It's hard to hear anything."

"That's okay. It's totally understandable. From what I can tell, you've suffered some head trauma." He unbuttoned his shirt, removed it, and used it to dab the wound.

She winced.

"Sorry," he said. "It's important that you tell me anything you remember so we can help piece together what happened to you."

"I woke up and it was dark. I didn't know where I was. Or who I was. I stumbled around for a bit."

She rubbed her right temple. "I heard a voice. Or I think I heard someone."

"Do you know if it was male or female?"

"I can't remember. I just know I was scared." She looked down. "And covered in blood. I found a place to hide. I remember looking up at the night sky. The stars and the moon were so bright, but I was so tired. I had to close my eyes. Next thing I knew it was light out and I saw you and your friend."

The rustling of boots on the trail caught his attention.

Tal appeared in the clearing. "Haven and the medics are three minutes out."

"I understand you don't remember anything. However, your name is Odessa, so that's what people will call you. Does the name feel familiar?"

"I can't say that it does."

That sucked. He couldn't imagine what it would be like to not know anything about his life. To not remember those he loved. His mama. His past. Even his ex-wife.

But especially Odessa.

"A police officer named Haven is about to come through those bushes. You know her. She's bringing with her medical professionals. We're going to take you to the hospital, get you checked out, and make sure you're safe."

"How do I know that I can trust you?"

"First, I'm a park ranger. It's my job to protect people out here. Haven's a cop, and she's good people," Thane said. "But I'll also call my mom. She's got some pictures of us from when we were kids. It might help ease your concern and maybe jog some memories."

"What about my family?" she asked. "I do have a family, don't I?"

"We'll talk all about that at the hospital." Thane palmed her cheek and smiled. "Haven and the paramedics are here." He rolled back onto his ankles to stand.

She grabbed his arm. "You're not going to leave me, are you?"

"Not if you don't want me to." He patted her bare leg.

"Will you come with me to the hospital?"

"I'll even ride in the ambulance with you." He nodded. "But you have to let these two check you out before they transport you. Okay?"

"You won't let anything happen to me?"

He took her hand and kissed her palm. "No. I promise you, I won't." Thane stepped aside, letting the EMTs in to do their work. He pulled Haven to the side and let out a long breath. "We need to get her off this mountain without Grant knowing."

"Why? We'll have to tell him we found her and maybe seeing him will bring her memory back." Haven cocked her head. "I need to know what she saw. I need answers."

"I know that. But I'd rather she have a full workup at the hospital before we introduce him into the mix. She's terrified. And he's a master manipulator."

"He's her fucking fiancé," Haven said. "Where do you think she will go when the doctors release her?" She glared. "And let's not forget she's a person of interest. Amnesia or not, she's the only link to what happened to her friends."

"Don't even go down that road with me," Thane said. "Look at her. No way in hell did she have anything to do—"

"Thane, I didn't say she was a suspect."

"You didn't have to." He planted both hands on his hips and glared. "Regardless, the best place for her is with me. Not Grant. You should be questioning him, especially after that damn press conference he held."

"Trust me, we'll have a nice chat with him, but

you can't rewrite history. Once she finds out she's engaged to another man, it will be her choice where she goes."

"Not if I have anything to say about it." And Thane was going to have a lot to say.

3

Odessa.

Everyone said that was her name.

Doctors, police officers, search and rescue, random people she came in contact with—and one very sexy park ranger.

There was something familiar about his intense, dark eyes and his kind, tender touch. Perhaps it was because he was the person who had found her and rode with her to the hospital. The one who held her hand when the nurse stuck her with needles and drew blood. The one who kept telling her that everything was going to be okay.

He'd also been the person to tell her she was alone in this world. That her parents had died a little over a year ago. Hearing those words tore open a hole in her heart. She was sure she had already felt that pain before, but now it engulfed her like the deep, dark forest filled with every scary monster that had ever lined the pages of a story.

Thane had been so kind, and she had to admit, there was something intimately recognizable about him. But the emotions he evoked confused her.

They were both warm and cold. Caring and distant.

But she didn't know what feeling to trust.

Her mind was mostly dark space with the occasional flash of light. Behind those lightning bolts were pieces of images, but she couldn't focus on them long enough to even know what they were.

Much less make sense of anything.

It was strange that she could function as a human. Knew about things. For example, she knew she absolutely hated pudding. The second the nurse had brought that vile stuff in, she pushed it away. However, she couldn't explain how she knew her taste buds would revolt. Or that she preferred diet soda to coffee. Loved chocolate of any kind. And her favorite meal was grilled chicken Caesar salad. She could eat that all day long and never get bored.

How she knew any of this but didn't know her own name or couldn't recognize her friends made her want to climb under the sheets and cry like a baby.

She stared out the little window from her private room. Thane, Haven, and Doctor Anita Reynolds were huddled outside her door.

Talk about giving her something to make her jittery over.

She'd been poked and prodded a dozen times. It felt as though half her body had been drained of all her blood. The doctors took X-rays and scans. They had stitched her up and told her they'd be back as soon as they had the results from all the tests.

But now the good doctor spoke with the sexy park ranger and the sweet cop before coming in to talk to the patient.

Odessa sighed, dropping her head back. She squeezed her eyes shut and desperately tried to remember what happened.

Nothing but darkness with the occasional image of her running from something.

An animal?

A voice?

All she knew was it was dark except for the bright moon and stars that had guided her as she ran. But when she glanced over her shoulder in her mind, she thought she saw a flash searing through the trees.

And heard a familiar sound.

"Sorry to disturb your rest," Dr. Reynolds said as she proudly strolled into the room. The woman carried herself with such confidence.

Odessa wondered if she ever had that kind of conviction. She blinked. The bright-white iridescent lights assaulted her vision like an out-of-control train. "It's okay," she said. "Have you gotten any of my test results back yet?"

"I have." The doctor sat on the edge of the bed. "You definitely have a concussion, but there isn't any swelling or brain bleed. So that's good news."

"So, why can't I remember anything?"

"I suspect whatever trauma you experienced, your mind is protecting you from it." The doctor patted her hand. "I'm recommending a specialist for you to speak with. A neurologist by the name of Jenna Chamber. She's dealt with a few cases like yours."

"I'm not sure what that means," Odessa mumbled.

"You've been through something terrible and two people are dead," Doctor Reynolds said. "Our mind is a complicated organ. Whatever happened, your brain is choosing to shut it out and the police need to chat with you."

"That man out there—Thane—he says those two women were my friends."

"They were." The doctor nodded. "And I'd like you to call me Anita because we were also friendly."

"We were?"

"You grew up in this town. You have deep ties to Fallport, bringing me to something else I need to discuss with you." Anita jerked her thumb over her shoulder. "Thane would like to be present for this discussion, but I will only bring him in if you want me to."

"He's been very kind to me."

"He's a good man. But you and he have an interesting history." Anita arched her brow. "What has he told you about that?"

"Nothing, really," Odessa said. "He mentioned something about his mom and her bringing pictures that might spark my memories."

"I only want you to do that under a session with the neurologist." Anita glanced over her shoulder. "Doctor Jenna Chamber is on her way down. She should be here any second. How do you feel about Thane being present?"

"I'm okay with it." Odessa nodded.

Anita pursed her lips and folded her arms.

"Is there something you're not telling me?"

"There's a lot we're not informing you of," Anita said. "There is a fine line between easing your mind back to reality, and info-dumping things on you that might be benign, but in actuality could be triggering. We want to—"

The door swung open and an unfamiliar—yet familiar—woman strolled in. Then again, nearly everyone gave off that vibe. "Good afternoon." The woman wasn't very tall. Maybe five-three. She wore her long dark hair in a bun at the nape of her neck. She had a stunning dark complexion with bright-blue eyes.

Odessa believed she had seen those eyes before, and a flare of jealousy filled her gut. She had no idea why, but it coated her belly and festered like a bad meal.

"I'm Doctor Chamber, but please, call me Jenna," the woman said with a smile that seemed genuine, but how was Odessa supposed to know.

"Do we know each other too?" Odessa asked. "Because I get the feeling we might have met."

"We have." Jenna lifted the chart from the end of the bed. "But only a couple of times and it was in passing. However, I want you to run with those feelings. Anita tells me that every time you've had a reaction to someone or something, it's been correct. That's good. It means your mind and all its memories are churning in your brain, searching for the one thing to help you unlock all those mysteries."

"If that's true, then why aren't I looking at someone I know and being flooded with my life?" Odessa asked with tears burning in her eyes.

"Unfortunately, I don't have the answer to that. And you'll soon learn, I don't have answers to a lot of questions you might have," Jenna said, setting the chart by Odessa's feet. "Why you've blocked out all your memories, we don't know. But years of experience tell me you're not ready to deal with whatever happened. My job is to get you there." The two doctors stole a glance.

That meant something.

Odessa sucked in a deep breath and waited for whatever news they had to share. She adjusted her pillow and sat up a little taller.

"Before we bring in our resident local police officer and Thane, we want to go over a couple of the medical tests," Anita said. "For the record, we have given them to Haven."

"Am I in trouble?" Odessa swallowed.

Jenna sat on the other side of the bed and took

her hand. "The police need to figure out what happened to your friends. Right now, you're the only link. But since you have no recollection, and there were date rape drugs in your system, you're being looked at as a person of interest, not a suspect."

"I don't know if that makes me feel better," Odessa said softly. "Or worse."

"My job is to help you explore your feelings and try to jog your memory in a way that doesn't overstimulate you," Jenna said. "I've told Officer Campbell that she can ask some probing questions, with the understanding that it might go absolutely nowhere."

"And Odessa has asked that Thane Bishop, the park ranger, be present. They do have a history, and she feels comfortable with him," Anita added.

"What about the—"

"We haven't had that conversation yet," Anita interrupted Jenna. "I wanted you to be present and Thane wants to be in the room."

"I'm sorry. I don't mean to be rude, but can we please not talk about me like I'm not sitting right here?" Odessa rubbed her temples. Every muscle ached. Her bones hurt. Her brain filled with flashes of nothing, if that made any sense.

It was maddening.

It boggled the mind that she knew so much and yet couldn't piece together a single thing about her past. Things and people either had a hint of recognition or they didn't. Emotions, both good and bad, filled her gut. She had no idea how to sort any of it.

"Why don't we bring Officer Campbell and the park ranger in." Jenna turned and made her way to the door.

Wonderful. More bits and pieces of her life would be spoon-fed to her by strangers.

"I don't care what *he* wants." Thane widened his stance, folded his arms, and glared. He absolutely knew he was in the wrong. Thane had no claim to Odessa. They were barely even friends anymore. But that didn't change the pit in his stomach.

The military had taught him to trust his instincts. He wanted to believe that his instincts were screaming at him that Grant was a piece of shit who couldn't be trusted.

Well, the piece of shit part was spot-on.

Everyone knew there was no love lost between

Grant and Thane. However, that didn't mean that Grant was a criminal.

"I can't keep Grant from seeing her," Haven said. "Once Weston is done with his interview, there is no logical reason for anyone to keep Grant from marching himself into that room."

"All I'm asking is for a little more time before we let him up here. Something doesn't feel right and I want to see her reaction to learning she possibly has a fiancé."

"Just because you didn't notice a ring on her finger Thursday night doesn't mean anything." Haven shook her head. "I wish I hadn't told you that we found her engagement ring at the lower ridge near the bodies. It doesn't make Grant a suspect and until we know more, we can't have you jumping to conclusions."

"Does he have a rock-solid alibi for the night?"

"Do you?" Haven asked with a little too much sarcasm. "Because both you and your mama were sound asleep isn't rock solid." She raised her hand. "What motive does he have in killing Chrissy and Sylvia?"

"They were in his way and Odessa was his real target."

"I'm seriously not having this conversation with

you." Haven heaved in a deep breath, glancing over her shoulder. "I understand your concern. This will be a tough case, especially with Odessa not remembering anything." She shifted her gaze. "Don't get your panties in a wad, but she's our best witness and our best—"

"Don't even fucking say it." Thane shook his head. "You can't for one second consider Odessa a suspect. What would she have to gain by killing her friends?"

"I'm a cop. I have to consider every possibility, whether I want to believe it or not. Right now, she's still a person of interest. I have more than one witness who says the girls were fighting. I want to rule her out, but we have to spend some time listening to all the players. That includes Grant." She jerked her chin toward the door. "However, it's made harder when she claims she doesn't remember anything."

"Claims? Are you kidding me right now? I know you read the toxicology report. She was fucking given a date rape drug."

"Thane. I am well aware of what was found in her system. That means we also have to think this could have been random and that's scary for different reasons. But if you keep tossing everything back in my face, I will stop allowing you access to intel." Haven curled her fingers around his biceps. "I'm only doing my job. Put yourself in my shoes for five seconds."

"No, thank you." He lifted his cap and raked his fingers through his hair. He absolutely understood the process. He simply didn't like it. "I'm sorry. I'm frustrated and I'm worried what Grant will do. Sadly, even more worried if he's not our guy."

"I am too, but I can't stop him from seeing her without a valid reason."

"Well, let's find one."

The door to Odessa's room opened and Jenna Chamber stuck her head out.

Thane groaned. When he'd learned Jenna would be the neurologist treating Odessa, he wanted to crawl under a rock. What were the odds that the one woman he'd had any kind of relationship with since moving back to Fallport would be Odessa's doctor.

Though calling what they had a relationship was a real stretch.

Jenna stuck her hands in her pockets and made her way into the hallway. She was a petite woman with striking blue eyes, dark hair, and a way too serious attitude. Not even a dry sense of humor.

However, she was brilliant, and they did have instant chemistry.

Only, that spark fizzled out quickly because they had absolutely nothing in common. Of course, Jenna had other reasons for ending their ridiculously short-lived affair.

That reason was now her patient.

"Hello, Thane." Jenna nodded. "Haven, always good to see you." She glanced over her shoulder. "Let's get right to it with some ground rules." She held up her hand when Thane opened his mouth. "Thane, you're only here because my patient has agreed. Although, I'm worried you might have manipulated that situation." She arched her perfect brow. One thing Thane had to admit—besides Jenna's intelligence—was her sheer natural beauty.

"I did nothing of the sort. I'm the one who found her, and we do have a history. I only want what's best for her."

"Because I know you genuinely care about Odessa and you might be able to help her regain memories, I'm going to allow it. But you have to follow my suggestions or we'll have a problem." She blew out a puff of air. "While she has no concrete memories, her brain is registering some recognition of people through emotions. That's promising. I want to keep working with that, through spoon-feeding her concepts and ideas about who she is. However, I don't want to frustrate her, so we need to do it so that she's not being quizzed or bombarded with your recollections of the past."

"I'm not sure I'm understanding what you mean," Thane said. Sometimes he felt like the dumbest person in the room when Jenna spoke. Part of her charm, which often made him chuckle.

But not today.

"Her memories are there, much like a word or name you can't recall, but it's on the tip of your tongue," Jenna said. "Trying too hard often makes it feel like that word or name slips deeper into obscurity. But if we leave it alone, it pops into our consciousness when we least expect it. Only, that's not really what's happening. Things in our mind are working to find it, like a computer working a software program in the background. We need to be that program, but I want it to be subtle."

"Okay. That makes sense." Thane appreciated the way Jenna described the situation. There were times she used words and phrases he couldn't understand. It drove him crazy.

"Odessa had a visceral response to me. While I wouldn't say she recoiled, I could see she questioned whether or not she could trust me. It was the same look she gave me the second time we met all those months ago." Jenna stuffed her hands in her pockets. "She suspected we might have had a connection; she just had no idea the circumstances or the history. What concerns me for Odessa is if her memory comes back rapidly, she might not have the coping skills to deal with it, which is why I want to ease her into all this with a few well-placed hints, a couple of really positive pictures of her past, and I need to watch her reaction to everyone who could be involved in what happened on that mountain."

"You're the doctor." Thane nodded. While he and Jenna had become oil and water in the bedroom and could barely be friends, she was an excellent neurologist. The best. He'd trust her with his life. "I can have my mom bring over some pictures from high school. Things like prom or even graduation. She was really happy then."

"Those will work." Jenna nodded.

"You know, I've seen similar situations in the military. I've known men who couldn't remember being tortured or the event that put them in the hospital. However, they never lost their entire identity. Why can't she remember anything?"

"The brain is a complicated organ and we don't

know very much about it," Jenna said. "If she remembers one thing, it could trigger a flood of memories, including that night. But we also have to consider that the head trauma could have affected her short-term memory. It's possible she never had the chance to process what she saw or did."

Thane held his breath and clenched his fists, keeping his words to himself. While Haven, Weston, and the rest of the police force had to look at all possibilities, Thane could only focus on one.

Grant.

He was the only one who made sense to Thane.

"I do have a few questions I need to ask her." Haven pointed to the room. "I won't be long and because I know Thane is going to ask, it's fine with me if he's there."

"All right. But please don't get her too worked up." Jenna turned on her heel and opened the door, waving her hand.

Thane made a beeline for Odessa's bedside. "How are you holding up?"

"I have no idea," Odessa said. "Everything is so foreign to me, and yet so familiar. I don't understand."

"Do you remember me?" Haven asked.

"Only from earlier when Thane found me."

Odessa dropped her head back on the pillow and immediately regretted it. The dull throb turned to a sharp pain and it went straight from her head right down to her toes.

"I need to ask you a few things." Haven pulled out a pad and pen. "What were you, Chrissy, and Sylvia fighting about?"

"I don't remember. I don't even remember going camping," Odessa said with a quivering lower lip. "Everything is so weird. Like the *Twilight Zone*. And how do I even know that's a television show, but not know a single thing about my life?"

Thane hated seeing her like this. The Odessa he used to know, the one he'd fallen in love with, was strong. Outspoken. She was the kind of woman who forged through doors. She made things happen, even when she was afraid.

Until fucking Grant happened. That man was a wrecking ball. He destroyed everything—and everyone—in his path.

"I can imagine that would be insanely frustrating," Haven said.

"You have no idea. I don't know any of these people. Nor do I remember anything about Fallport. But when we walked down the trail, I knew my way. As if I'd done it before."

"Because you have," Thane said.

Odessa rubbed her temples. "That makes no sense."

"It's not uncommon for people with amnesia to know some things and not others," Jenna said. "What I'd like you to do is focus on the reactions your body and mind have to the questions Haven's about to ask. Take your time and let the questions settle with those emotions and that might trigger a physical memory. If it doesn't, try to hold on to those feelings. File them somewhere so you can pull them all together and possibly piece events back in place when you're faced with another one."

Thane patted her leg and smiled.

"I'll try, but it's all so confusing." Odessa nodded.

"I'd like to show you some pictures and I want you to tell me what you know or remember about them." Haven pulled out her cell and tapped the screen, staring at it momentarily. Her eyes widened and she pursed her lips.

Thane didn't like that expression. He wanted to ask what brought the contemplative expression but now wasn't the time.

Haven swiped, then turned the phone, holding it up to Odessa.

At least it was an image Odessa should recognize.

Odessa squinted as she took the cell into her shaky hand. "It's the same thing. I feel like I should know these people. There is a hint of recognition, but I can't form names or memories."

"What kind of emotions do they give you?" Jenna asked.

"Warm. Friendly," Odessa said softly. "But I can't recall anything." She blinked, sucking in a deep breath. "Are these… are these… my friends who died?"

"When do you remember last seeing them?" Haven asked.

Thane shifted his stare and shot daggers at Haven. Dumbass fucking trick.

Odessa brought the cell closer, as if to study it. She bit down on her lower lip. Once again, it quivered. Her hand trembled. "I'm sorry. I wish I knew. I want to help. I want to know what happened. My memories seem to start when I woke up in the woods in the dark." She glanced up. "I'm sorry. I really am."

At least Thane knew she wasn't lying.

"What about this man?" Haven leaned over,

wiggled her finger at her screen, and swiped. "Do you recognize him?"

Odessa's eyes narrowed. Her breath hitched. She pressed her head farther back on the pillow. "I don't know. I honestly don't know," she whispered.

He knew Odessa. He understood her facial expressions and that furrowed brow could only mean one thing.

Fear.

But did she know why she was afraid of Grant? That was the million-dollar question.

"What are you feeling right now?" Jenna inched closer. She glanced at the machine checking Odessa's vitals. Her pulse had increased ever so slightly.

"Same familiar emotions. As if I know him, but I can't place him. It's like he has a face I might have seen before, but I just don't remember," Odessa said. "Who is he? Why should I know him? Please just tell me. I can't stand all this a second longer."

"His name is Grant Mercer." Haven tucked her pad and paper into her pocket and took her cell. "Name jog your memory at all?"

"No more than when Thane or you told me your names. But I'm starting to think everyone in this town has some tie to me." Odessa hugged her middle. "I'm tired of riddles. Can someone just tell me who he is?"

When frustration settled into her bones, at least the Odessa he dated, she tended to get a little snippy. Sometimes downright angry or mean. Or both.

Thane absolutely believed she had no idea who or what Grant was to her and that posed so many different problems.

But why wasn't she expressing the alarm he'd triggered? That didn't settle well with Thane.

"He's your fiancé," Jenna said. "And he's downstairs waiting to see you."

Just hearing the word *fiancé* made Thane's stomach churn.

Odessa's jaw flopped open. She grabbed her left hand and thumbed her ring finger. She glanced between him, the doctor, Haven, and back to him. "Why didn't anyone tell me this sooner?" She drew her lips into a tight line, holding Thane's gaze for a good ten seconds. "Why didn't you tell me this when you told me about my parents? Why would you keep it from me? That's not fair. Obviously, something bad happened to me and you all are treating me like I did something." She glanced down. "And why aren't I wearing an engagement ring?"

"All we're doing is trying to protect you," Thane said. "And find answers."

"Maybe my memories will come back if I'm with my family," she said with a fair amount of disdain and disgust, which sounded more like the Odessa he knew a week ago. "With the man whom I chose to be with."

Her words cut Thane to the bone. "Don't you need to interview him?" He cocked his head, staring at Haven, knowing full well that Weston was already doing the honors.

She nodded. "I'll go down and chat with him now and then send him up."

"Please do that," Odessa said. "I want to see him. Maybe he's exactly what I need to remember, and can someone please tell me where my ring is?"

"We don't know," Haven said. "You weren't wearing one."

Thane was thrilled that Haven tackled that one. Odessa might not remember anything, but her personality was coming out in spades. At least the old Odessa was and she was like a dog with a bone when it came to stuff like that.

"In the meantime, I'd like you to rest." Jenna

patted her leg. "I'm going to be keeping you overnight for observation. Thane, why don't you walk me out."

The last thing Thane wanted to do was leave Odessa, but what choice did he have? Her doctor demanded she rest and he had no right to keep fucking Grant from seeing her, no matter what he thought.

He took Odessa's hand and kissed it. "I'll leave my number with the nurse. You can call me anytime. Later, I'll bring a new phone for you."

"I'm sure that won't be necessary."

"It's not a big deal." He smiled. "Get some rest. I'll see you later." He followed Jenna and Haven out the door and back into the hallway before Odessa could protest further.

Jenna stuffed her hands in her pockets. "I'm sure I'm not the only one who noticed Odessa having a mild negative reaction to Grant's image. Does someone want to tell me why that might be?"

"I believe she might have broken off the engagement, but I can't be sure," Thane said. He left out the part about Haven finding the ring by the dead bodies. That wasn't his place, but it wasn't lost on him that she was keeping her trap shut. "And then there's what I think about the relationship, but you already know my thoughts on that."

"Yup. I sure do." Jenna sighed. "Her reactions could simply be that they had a fight the last time they spoke or that she was caught off guard since we kept that from her for a few hours." She held up her hand. "Her pulse didn't go wild, nor did her blood pressure. It was a slight increase. Nothing I would consider cause for alarm. But there was also an interesting shift in her personality. This reunion could tell us something."

"Maybe I should stay," Thane said.

"I don't think that would be helpful for a number of reasons," Jenna said, turning her attention to Haven. "Is Grant a suspect in the murder of her friends?"

"No." Haven lowered her gaze. "Weston finished with the interview." She pulled out her cell and waved. "I got word while interviewing Odessa that he has an airtight alibi."

"You've got to be kidding me," Thane mumbled.

"I'm not," Haven said. "He was at car show about an hour away. He'd checked into his hotel Friday at four. Locals there did a solid and spoke to three witnesses. He drove back the second he heard the news."

"That's convenient." Thane lifted off his cap, folded it, and tucked it in his back pocket.

"Since we're on the subject." Haven tapped her cell. "Weston also mentioned that Grant stated on Thursday evening that *he* called off his engagement to Odessa. According to him, she wasn't happy and threw a bottle of wine at him. My husband says he's got a black eye."

"I don't believe that for one second." Thane raked his fingers through his unruly hair. "While Grant often treated her like she was beneath him, I don't see him letting her go and I sure as shit don't believe she'd hurl a bottle at him. If he's got a black eye, it didn't happen then."

"That picture I showed her, Weston just took." Haven arched a brow. "It shows the damage to his face. Weston's going to poke around and see if anyone saw him with that mark on his face Friday. Grant also says there is a big stain on his living room carpet. He's painting a picture that lately Odessa has had some anger issues, which is one of the reasons he decided it was time to call it quits."

"That's bullshit," Thane said behind a tight jaw.

Haven raised her hand. "I'm just repeating what I know. Regardless, Grant has an alibi."

"He could have driven back in the middle of the night," Thane said.

"That crossed Weston's mind." Haven nodded. "But Grant had an answer for that." She arched a brow. "And her name is Leslie Anne Seymore."

"He was fucking his IT manager?" Thane folded his arms across his chest and swallowed the bile that slammed the back of his throat. Leslie Anne had been looking for her sugar daddy for as long as Thane could remember. It was pathetic, but only because the woman had so much going for her. She was intelligent, beautiful, and she commanded a room.

But for whatever reason, she wanted a man to take care of her every need. A year ago, she had her sights set on old man Crenshaw. When that didn't work out, she went after his son, Todd. But that didn't last very long when she realized being the wife of a rancher was hard work, no matter how rich they were.

"According to this very long text from Weston, nothing happened between Grant and Leslie Anne until after he called it quits with Odessa." Haven stuffed her cell back in her pocket. "Weston is on his way up with Grant and suggested that Thane disappear."

"I couldn't agree more." Jenna actually took her hand out of her lab coat and curled her fingers around Thane's biceps, giving it a little squeeze. "When she found out about Grant, she directed all that anger of not knowing at you. She senses all that history. Thing is, I know that story, and not just through your eyes."

"What are you saying?" Thane asked. In the past, Jenna always thought that Thane had been obsessed with Odessa. That he'd still been in love with her and had never let her go. That until he either admitted that or walked away, he'd never be able to move on with his life.

He laughed at the concept.

Only, Jenna was right.

"I've seen them out a few times having dinner with various people. I saw how controlling he can be. As her doctor, I promise I'll keep an eye on that and help guide her through this without his manipulations." Jenna smiled. It wasn't something she did often, but it was sweet and genuine when she did.

"I appreciate that, but let me ask you this," Thane said. "What's going to happen when you release her tomorrow? Technically, she lives with that asshole."

"We'll cross that bridge tomorrow." Jenna pointed toward the elevator. "Go grab some food. I'll text you when he's gone."

Thane did need to check in with his mother. His buddies busted his balls all the time about being a mama's boy at nearly forty. He didn't give a shit. His mother was his world, especially after losing his dad. He'd do anything for his mom and right now, she was worried sick about Odessa. "All right. But just remember, my patience runs thin real quick."

4

Odessa stared at a man whom she was supposed to love. He was handsome enough with his perfectly styled hair. Freshly shaved face. And his fancy clothes.

But she found it odd that her first thought when she laid eyes on him was that he wasn't Thane.

Her second thought was Grant reminded her of a cold fish. She expected this Grant person to waltz into the room, take her into his arms, kiss her passionately, and make her feel safe and warm.

None of that happened.

Instead, he stood at the edge of her bed with a death grip on the footboard as if she might hurl herself from the mattress like a possessed creature, stabbing him with a corkscrew.

Not to mention, there were no warm and fuzzy feelings on her part. Her blood raced through her system as if it were on fire—and not in a good way. Her skin prickled.

But why was she angry? Why did she want to tell this man to fuck off?

He inched closer to the side of the bed and took her hand. "You don't remember anything?"

Her dry, scratchy eyes burned with waterless tears. "The only memories I have are from when I was found to this moment." She stared at their intertwined fingers, searching for a hint of recognition. A fleeting sensation that would catapult her into a memory with this man. But all she got was a jolt of electricity and she wanted to yank her hand away. She wanted to tell him to get out. To leave her alone and to never come back.

But again, she had no idea why. She blinked, shifting her gaze to his almond-colored eyes. They had a coldness to them, even though they were pretty.

"So, you don't remember our fight on Thursday? Or moving out?" He touched the side of his face, rubbing his temple by a small cut. A large dark-purple bruise covered his eye.

"I'm sorry. I don't. What happened?" she asked,

even though she wanted to know why he fixated on that and not her dead friends. On who attacked her. On who gave her a date rape drug. It seemed odd.

Grant glanced over his shoulder. "Is it okay if I tell her how I remember things?"

Odessa swallowed. Hard. Jenna had told her to hold on to every feeling. Every emotional reaction and file it somewhere in her brain. To think of these feelings as memories. So far, everyone gave her mostly good feelings. Or, at worst, a mixed bag of warmth and confusion.

Like Thane. Deep down, she knew she could trust him. Or should trust him even though a part of her felt like he'd somehow wronged her in life.

With Jenna, it seemed more like they sat on the opposite side of the cafeteria in high school.

Grant grated on her nerves. She didn't trust him. Something told her that he would lie to get what he wanted. But he also made her heart beat faster. Gave her sweaty palms—out of fear. Her entire body warned her that this man was not who she wanted to be with, but she had no valid reason for believing that.

"Odessa, would you like to hear his version?" Jenna held up her hand when Grant opened his mouth. "I want to interject here that two people will experience the same event but could have a different recollection of what transpired. No offense, Grant, but your perceptions of any event are tainted by your point of view and your emotions. Odessa doesn't have much to go on here and it's obvious to me that whatever happened before the camping trip was incredibly emotional. So, it would be helpful if you could try to speak in facts and leave out any dramatizations, your personal feelings, or even commentary on what you believe Odessa might have been thinking or feeling at the time."

"I suppose I can do that." Grant pursed his lips. It was a strange look, and Odessa couldn't be sure what it meant, but she believed his mind was turning over ways to control this situation.

Why she thought that, she had no idea.

Grant sat on the edge of the bed, still holding her hand, though she had to admit there was a distance between them. It wasn't the same kind and caring gesture as when Thane did it.

"You see, we've been having problems for a while," Grant said. "You'd become… unhappy with some things in our relationship, I guess is the best way to put it."

"Grant, that's interjecting Odessa's emotions into the story," Jenna said.

Odessa's heart jumped up to her throat. It wasn't out of fear, but out of jubilation.

It was as if it were celebrating Grant getting that one right.

Odd sensation.

He glanced in Jenna's direction. "I don't know how to keep this impartial. It was a difficult night."

"I want to hear this," Odessa said. "I'm okay with a little interjection."

Jenna nodded. "Go ahead and tell her from your perspective."

"All right." He patted Odessa's hand. "We had been fighting a fair amount about a lot of different topics. It was getting to the point that we fought every day and I was tired of it. I wanted to go to counseling. You refused."

"I need to ask something," Jenna said. "Are you sure that Odessa never sought counseling before?"

"Oh, she has. When her parents died." Grant nodded like a bobblehead. "She saw one for a few months but then stopped going. When things started to get bad for us, I suggested couples therapy, but she refused."

"When was that?" Jenna asked.

"About the time we sold her parents' house." Grant slumped his shoulders. "I thought it was too soon, though I did believe it was good for her to move out."

"So, we broke up because I wouldn't go to therapy?" she asked with a shaky voice. She resented that fear bubbling up into her words. That it was her entire state. Not knowing anything about her life was going to make her crazy. But the worst part was she didn't believe a damn word he said.

"That was one of the reasons," Grant said. "These last couple of months you've really struggled with your temper. You take your anger and frustration out on me. I've tried to be understanding." He squeezed her hand. "You've been through so much." He tapped his temple. "But this was too much."

"I did that to you?" She sat up, leaning closer, squinting, trying to force a memory. Trying to pluck it from obscurity.

Nothing.

The only thing that registered was confusion.

And fear.

She believed that whatever was once between them was over. But what didn't make sense was the slight tremble that filled her insides.

"Unfortunately, you tossed a wine bottle at me when I told you that you made a mistake by canceling a repeat customer to take on a bigger client," Grant said. "After you hit me, I asked you to pack your bags and leave. You did. This is the first time I've seen you since then, but you have texted and called."

"What have I messaged you?" Odessa asked.

"Nothing very nice." Grant lowered his chin. "Lots of name-calling. Threats."

Odessa solidly believed this was all a lie. But she honestly had nothing to back that up with.

"All I want for you is to get better. I will help you any way I can. I wanted to bring you some of your favorite things from home, only I don't know where you took all your belongings." He patted her thigh. "I've asked Weston to check around. If we find your stuff, I'll make sure you get your things."

"Thank you."

"The police will catch whoever did this to you and your friends," Grant said. "They've promised me they will have an officer on this floor at all times and once you're released, they will make sure there is an increased police presence wherever you are. But I don't trust that. I have a friend who owns a security firm. I've hired him. He'll have a man here on this floor to make sure nothing happens."

"I'm sorry, but that's against hospital policy," Jenna said. "He can't stay."

Grant frowned. "Okay. I guess the cop at the door will have to do. But when you come home, I'll have a bodyguard." He leaned over and kissed her forehead. "I need to head back to work. I'll be in touch later." He nodded toward Jenna and then was out the door in a flash.

Odessa reached for her water and slurped on the straw. There was no base context for that conversation. And all she felt was relief that it was over. "Please don't ask me how I feel." She glared at Jenna. "Or what emotions I'm processing."

"Unfortunately, that's my job." Jenna pulled the chair closer, sat down, and rested the patient chart in her lap. "My goal is to help you gain your memories. My concern is how those memories flood your brain and what that might do to you emotionally. Especially when it comes to what happened to you and your friends out there on that mountain." Jenna glanced to the ceiling. "I also have to deal with the police. Two women are dead. You're the key to unlocking what happened and you might still be in danger." She pointed toward the door. "That's why there is an armed officer at the door."

"I have to wonder if I'm also a suspect." Sucking down the last of the water, Odessa set the cup back on the tray.

"I'm not going to lie to you. The cops have no choice but to consider that," Jenna said.

"You knew me before all this. Was I an angry person?"

"I didn't know you well, and we weren't friends. I have no idea," Jenna said. "What I can tell you is that everyone gets mad."

"Does everyone toss a bottle at their boyfriend?"

"That depends on what happened leading up to the event." Jenna leaned forward, resting her elbows on the chart. "I want to do what is called reminiscence therapy. Thane will bring images from his mother's photo album that represent a positive time in your life. Maybe we can stimulate some memories."

"Why not start with pictures of me and Grant?"

"Besides the negative physiological effect he's having on you? The night before you lost your memory, you and he had a life-changing event. I don't want to trigger you into what happened. I know that's what the police want, but you're my patient, and I believe easing you into it is best." Jenna flipped open her chart and jotted something down. "You've known Thane and his mom since you were a little girl. I'm sure he can find a photograph that will bring only joyful memories." She closed the chart and lifted her gaze. "Don't stress if it doesn't happen right away. The mind is a powerful organ and there is a reason it doesn't want you to remember."

"Do me a favor and stop staying that shit. Especially the way you say it. Drives me crazy."

Jenna laughed. "I don't blame you. When I dated Thane, he used to tell me I sounded like a walking encyclopedia, and not in a smart way. I'll work on it."

Odessa's heart thumped like a jackhammer. Jealousy coursed through her veins. It was strong. Powerful. Like a bull charging at a matador.

But why?

"You and Thane?" Odessa asked.

"That was unprofessional of me," Jenna said. "I'm so sorry."

"Please don't be. This is one of the most normal conversations I've had since I got here. Will you tell me more?" None of this felt normal. Not that Odessa knew what normal was. She had no baseline for it. All she knew was uncertainty and darkness. Or maybe it was more like a Gaussian blur.

"There isn't much to tell," Jenna said. "I met him a few months after he came back to town. We went out a couple of times and quickly learned we don't have much in common."

"Is it weird that I don't believe you're his type?"

"No," Jenna said. "But can you elaborate on that?"

Odessa dropped her head back and groaned. "No. At least not in a concrete way and what I see as the perfect woman for that man makes me look like a loon."

"Like I said before, you've known him your entire life. You were close friends growing up. You dated. You definitely have an idea of who he'd be attracted to."

"For someone who's told everyone else not to hint at my past life on a regular basis"—Odessa rolled her head—"you're doing a lot of that right now. I feel this isn't a girl-to-girl chat, but a doctor trying to get her patient to remember something. Anything."

"I don't want the cops working you over trying to get information from you. I certainly don't want Thane bombarding you with one-sided information." Jenna waggled her finger. "Because that's what he would do. I want to control a little bit how the information comes at you. Besides, I have nothing to gain. The cops? They want something from you. I get it. That's important information and I want them to have it."

"And Thane? What does he want from me?" Odessa held her breath. A flash of a faint image crash-landed like a fuzzy old motion picture in her mind. She could barely make out two images. Two young kids. They were maybe eight or ten. They were running in a field. Laughing.

And then, just as quickly as it came, it was gone.

It wasn't enough of a memory to say anything. If it happened again, she'd tell Jenna.

"Ultimately, he wants you to be happy and safe," Jenna said.

"I take it he doesn't like Grant, does he?"

"There is no love lost between those two men." Jenna nodded. "The feeling is mutual."

"Does that have to do with me?"

"Not entirely, no," Jenna said. "But now we have to circle back to your reactions to seeing Grant."

Odessa sighed, dropping her head back. "I have

no basis for this, but I don't believe what he said about our breakup."

Jenna stood, closing the gap. She flipped open the patient chart, thumbing through the pages. "I have your entire medical history here and I'm guessing you kept this from Grant." She turned the chart, tapping her finger on one of the pages. "You stopped seeing a therapist a while back. However, on Thursday, you called and scheduled an appointment for next week. I find that interesting. If it's okay with you, I'd like that therapist to stop by before I release you tomorrow."

"Absolutely." Odessa wanted to speak with anyone who could give her straight answers. "Can I ask you a crazy question?"

"There is no such thing."

Odessa chuckled. "Where am I going to go tomorrow? I don't think I want to go home with Grant and can I say no to him?"

"If you don't feel comfortable going with Grant, I'm sure we can find other arrangements. I'll speak to Haven and Thane about it." Jenna hung the chart at the end of the bed. "Thane will be back up with his mom in a little bit. She's a lovely woman. Until then, I want you to rest."

"Thank you, Jenna."

"If you need me, tell the nurses. They will get me." Jenna nodded, then disappeared through the door.

Odessa lowered the bed a little, closed her eyes, and did her best to pull up the image of the two kids running through a meadow. Only this time, they were teenagers. The image was still fuzzy, but it gave her a sense of belonging. A sense of peace.

The boy had long wavy hair, almost to his shoulders. He paused, plucked a flower from the ground, and gently placed it the girl's… in Odessa's hair. The young man smiled before leaning in and brushing his lips over her mouth.

Odessa touched her lips. It was as if she'd felt it in real time. The warmth of that boy's embrace. The safety net his love provided.

And it was love.

But was it a real memory, or was she channeling something she'd seen on the television hours earlier? Or was her mind simply torturing her because it needed something to fill the utter darkness and emptiness that had been created?

Whatever this vision was, she held on to it with all her might. She needed something that wrapped her heart and soul with hope.

5

Thane paced in the hallway. He knew his mother could get in and out of a car service all by herself. While her autoimmune disorder was active, she was getting around well enough.

But he should have gotten in his truck, driven the fifteen miles, and picked her up himself instead of letting his mama talk him into eating a meal.

His stomach could have waited.

A deep familiar voice caught his attention. He paused and glanced over his shoulder.

Fucking Grant Mercer and hound dog Rufus.

Thane didn't know which man was worse.

"I hear you're the one who found Odessa." Grant stopped five paces away. He wore a freshly pressed blue button-down shirt. Dark pleated slacks. Shiny fancy shoes. His hair was parted and styled like he belonged on the pages of a fashion magazine.

Even Thane had to admit that Grant was a handsome man. His only problem was he had no soul. No heart.

"And I hear you were with another woman." Thane cocked a brow. He knew he shouldn't goad Grant. But he couldn't help himself. It kept him from sucker punching the jerk. That wouldn't solve anything. It would only get Thane in trouble and a long lecture from his mother.

Neither thing he needed.

"You don't know what you're talking about." Grant shook his head. "You know nothing of my life or how things were with me and Odessa."

"I know you're an asshole who doesn't deserve her." Thane planted his hands on his hips and puffed out his chest. He wasn't normally one for pissing contests, but Grant brought out the worst in him. "I know you controlled every aspect of her life right up until she decided to take it back on Thursday. I bet you didn't like that."

Grant snorted. "Not that I owe you an explanation, but I'm the one who broke up with her. I'm the one who asked her to pack up and leave. She didn't like it and she did this." Grant winced as he pointed to his eye. "She sent me numerous threatening texts. I could show you if you'd like."

Thane wouldn't believe them even if he saw the time stamp. Grant was a smart man with way too much money. He could make things happen if he wanted to.

Besides, Odessa's cell was missing.

"I don't know what kind of game you're playing here," Thane said. "Or what part you had in Odessa—"

"Stop right there, pal," Grant said. "Don't you dare go and accuse me of hurting Odessa. I loved her."

Loved? He was already using the term in past tense? What an asshole.

"She was my world and I tried to hold on to our relationship. You don't know what goes on behind closed doors. You have no idea what I went through with her or how she's changed. All I want to do is help her through whatever this is," Grant said.

"You're a fucking piece of work," Thane mumbled.

"No, you are. You're so blind with envy that you're willing to come at me—allege that I could have killed two innocent women—instead of focusing on the real problem," Grant said.

"Oh yeah. And what's that?"

"Finding out what happened to those girls." Grant let out a long breath. "The cops are clueless. Rufus and his men could figure this out faster."

Thane eyed Rufus. He was ex-military with a decent record. He wasn't the worst man in the world, but he seemed to have blind loyalty to Grant.

Something that Thane didn't understand.

And he couldn't stop Grant from hiring the man to check into things, if that was what he was really doing. "Just stay out of the cops' way. They do know what they're doing."

"Oh really." Grant laughed. "That's why it took our local police department how many years to solve what happened to Winslet's parents. Or how about Pandora's rapist? Hmmm. Yeah. If our cops are so good at their jobs, why didn't they arrest those idiots when those crimes happened?"

Thane wasn't about to get into this argument with Grant, because it wasn't the kind of argument he could win. Thane would not waste his breath. "Do what you have to but don't fuck with the investigation and stay away from Odessa. She's not your fiancée anymore."

Grant inched closer. "That may be true, but she has nowhere to go and no matter what she said or did to me, I'm not going to let her walk out of here alone."

Thane puffed out his chest. "You won't have to. She's staying with me."

"That's not going to happen." Grant smiled and strode toward the main doors, which swished open as his mother wobbled in, thankfully using her cane.

Thane rushed to his mother's side, grateful that all Grant did was say hello. "Let me take that." Thane kissed his mother's cheek and grabbed the tote bag. "Damn, Ma, what do you have in here?"

"A scrapbook, a couple of your high school yearbooks, and some home cooking for my Odessa. I made her favorite." His mother's lips curved into that all-knowing smile she had. Then she winked.

"Ma, no offense, but if Odessa doesn't remember me, she ain't gonna remember your lobster mac and cheese with your famous oatmeal vanilla chip cookies either." He looped his arm around his mom and guided her toward the elevator.

"Speak like a grown man, for Pete's sake." His mother lifted her cane and waved it out in front of them. "You know how I feel about words like ain't and gonna."

He chuckled. "Those words are now in the dictionary."

"I don't care. They're not proper and I raised you better," she said. "I'd rather you swear like a truck driver." She pursed her lips. "Which you do all the time anyway."

"Yes, ma'am." He pressed the up button.

Thane had been what his parents called a miracle baby. His dad was nearly forty-five, and his mom had been thirty-six when Thane had been conceived. His folks had tried for ten years to have a second child. They'd done everything they could, including spending a small fortune, and they had all but given up when they found out his mom was pregnant.

When he'd been a small boy, he loved that his older brother was more like an uncle. He enjoyed all the attention from his parents for himself, and they lathered him in love. He soaked it up like it was sunscreen being spread over his pale skin on the hottest of summer days.

But as he got older, he often wished for a younger brother or sister. Or that Asher, his older brother, was closer in age. Not for his parents, but for himself, because there were times in his childhood that being the only kid at home since he'd been eight was damn fucking lonely. He loved his parents—and Asher. They were awesome. His folks attended every sports event. Every school event. They were by his side when it mattered—and when it didn't.

Asher came home when he could. That was until he met his wife and took over her family winery out in California.

He loved his family more than he could ever express. He loved them so much that he had their names tattooed on his body—including his brother and his two boys.

However, the realization that they were all he had hit him hard. At thirty-eight, he didn't believe he'd ever have children of his own. Not that it wasn't possible—because he was the miracle baby—but because he'd first have to find the right girl and the reality was he'd let her slip through his fingers.

Ding.

The elevator doors slid open.

"I hope you're not the one who gave Grant that black eye?" His mom stepped into the small space, turned, and glared. "I don't care that he's a jerk, I don't—"

"According to him, Odessa smacked him with a wine bottle."

His mom grinned. "Well, good fucking for her," she said under her breath.

"Why don't you tell me how you really feel."

"I just did." She lifted her chin. "And since we're on the subject, I'll just say it. You belong with that girl."

Thane pressed the button and leaned against the wall. In the past, he'd deny it. He'd tell his mom that Odessa had made her choice and he'd moved on.

Only, if that were true, he'd have a girlfriend.

"Cat got your tongue?" His mom poked his foot with her cane.

He laughed. "No. Just don't feel like having the same discussion."

"Does that mean you're finally agreeing with me?" His mom lifted her chin, meeting his gaze. "And perhaps willing to do something about it?"

"She'd have to first remember me, and second, want to have something to do with me, and I fear the latter isn't ever going to happen when her memory finally does come back."

"Please explain why." His mama raised her cane, and when she did that, it was always best to shut his trap. "And don't go and tell me it's because you both broke each other's hearts at one time or another."

"But it's true," he said. "She wouldn't move away from Fallport. I was going from one base to the next, one deployment to the next, and she couldn't handle it. That didn't feel like love to me. Broke my heart, and I, in turn, broke hers when I married someone else."

"Speaking of your ex-wife, I got a very nice phone call from her the other day. She was always so sweet. As exes go, she's a good one."

"She's not the worst, that's for sure."

"Except for the open marriage thing." His mother chuckled, shaking her head. "That, I will never understand."

Thane smiled. "I did—do—love Tonia. She's a good person. We just weren't meant to be together."

"Because you're meant to—"

"Let's not beat a dead horse, Mama," he said as the elevator doors opened. "Remember, Odessa won't know you. She might have what the doctor is calling emotional memories—feelings tied to seeing you—but try not to bombard her with stuff from her childhood. Let's pick one or two pictures and tell her a nice story about something from her past. Let her ask questions. We shouldn't stay too long. She needs her rest."

"You're not going to stay here with her tonight?"

"Doc says it's not a good idea."

"Odessa needs you." His mom wobbled down the corridor. She was a proud woman. She never complained. When her illness got the better of her, she put on a smile and continued with her day. If it got to the point she couldn't, she shrugged her shoulders and still lifted her chin, telling him that there were worse things in the world. Her spirit was strong. Her resolve even stronger.

He tried not to let her see how much it broke his heart.

His father had died suddenly. Without warning. It had been a shock. He hadn't been prepared. He never got the chance to say goodbye. He wouldn't let that happen with his mom. Sadly, he knew her days were numbered. Her doctors told her she could have many years left.

But they might not be good ones.

"And I'll be here for her." He rested his hand on his mother's elbow, guiding her toward Odessa's room. A police officer diligently stood at the door. That was both good and bad. He was there for her protection.

But he was also there because Odessa was a person of interest.

A possible suspect.

That made his blood boil.

He nodded to the officer and opened the door.

Odessa turned her head and gave him a weak smile. She adjusted herself higher in the bed, arranging the blanket. "This must be your mother," she said softly.

No hint of recognition. The only thing he saw was the perpetual sadness etched in her pale-blue eyes.

He nodded. "You grew up calling her Mama Gayle."

Odessa squinted, raising her finger to her temple as if she were trying to extract a memory. Or at least that's what he thought she was doing.

"I brought you some homemade food," his mom said. "When you were in high school, this was one of your favorite meals."

Thane rolled the large reclining chair over for his mother to sit in before setting the bag of food on the tray. He reached in and pulled out a sealed bowl.

"Is that lobster mac and cheese?" Odessa sat up taller. "I don't remember anything about being a teenager, but something tells me I loved that meal."

"You did." His mom leaned forward, taking Odessa's hand. "On game days, whether it be football or lacrosse, you'd come over and help me make this."

"I wish I could remember just one thing about my life." Odessa opened the lid and took the fork he handed her, shamelessly digging in and taking a massive bite. "Oh my God. This is delicious."

"I'm glad you like it."

Odessa leaned back. Her eyes glassed over and she sighed. "Jenna keeps telling me to file all these emotional memories, and I do feel like I should know about this meal—about you—but I don't."

"Don't stress over it, dear." His mother smiled that sweet smile of hers. The one that used to make all his pain and sadness disappear when he was a small boy. "Thane, why don't you pull out the scrapbook and show her some pictures."

"Sure thing, Ma." He set the bag on the other chair, sat on the edge of the bed, and opened the book to a random page. He chuckled.

"What's so funny?" Odessa asked.

"Me," he said, shaking his head. "And my hair." He lifted the book. "I'll never forget the day I had to cut my hair when I joined the Marines. I don't know who was more devastated. Me or you."

Odessa dropped the fork. It first landed on her chest, then tumbled to the floor with a thud. She reached out with a shaky finger. "That boy is you?"

"I was almost a man in that picture." He cocked his head.

"It was your seventeenth birthday," his mother said. "That does not make for a man."

"Close enough, Ma."

"And that's me?" Odessa yanked the book from his hand, shifting her gaze between him and the few pictures on the page.

"It is." He tapped the page. "And that big guy is my dad."

"Minus that unruly hair my son refused to cut, he looked just like his father," his mom said with pride.

"I remember you," Odessa said. "I mean, I don't remember any of this. But that hair." She traced her finger over the image. "I remember all that hair."

Thane's breath caught in his throat. His heart dropped to his toes. "What do you mean?"

"Earlier, I had this image pass through my mind. Actually two. One was of two young kids running through a meadow. But then it changed to an image like this one, only in the same meadow." A single tear rolled down her cheek. "I know the girl in that field was me and now I know the boy was you. We were holding hands. You stopped and picked up a flower and put it in my hair. Then you…" She brought her fingers to her lips. "Was that real? Did I remember something?"

He reached out and wiped the tear away. "Yeah. You did."

"Jenna told me we dated." Odessa lifted the page but didn't turn it. "How old were we and when did we break up?"

"That's a long story and I'm not sure it's good for me to bombard you with—"

"Tell me. I need to know my history," she said with a shaky voice. She stared at him with wide eyes filled with uncertainty and desperation. "Do you have any idea what it's like not to know who you are? Where you come from? Or who to trust? I woke up in the woods, hurt, terrified, and with blood on me. I have no idea what happened to friends I don't remember. Please, I need to piece together my life. I'm begging."

"Why don't you turn the page and see if it sparks anything while I go find Jenna and see what she says. She's going to want to know you remembered something."

"I'll ring for her." Odessa hit the nurse call button. "But until she comes, you'll tell me a few things about my life. I don't care what they are. But I want something concrete."

"Okay." He let out a long breath. He couldn't go on torturing Odessa. It was cruel. Jenna could be mad at him all she wanted. He didn't care. If Odessa wanted a few pieces of her past, he'd give her some good ones.

Odessa held her breath. Knowing she'd had one real memory wasn't enough to make her a whole person. It didn't even make her a real person. However, it did give her hope. So much hope her heart bristled with the kind of excitement that a small child experienced on Christmas morning. It was bursting with all the possibilities.

"I'm waiting." She glanced between Thane and

his sweet mother, Gayle. She had the kindest eyes and warmest smile. Something about her gave Odessa a sense of safety.

And belongingness.

It was the first time that Odessa felt as though someone didn't want something from her.

While they treated her well, all the doctors still had an agenda.

The cops certainly had an agenda.

Even Thane had an agenda, even though he seemed to care more about her recovery than the man who claimed to have loved her enough to put a ring on her finger.

She struggled to believe she tossed a wine bottle at Grant's face. She didn't doubt she was angry. Heat prickled her skin the second he walked into the room. However, she didn't see herself as a violent person.

Yet, she didn't know one fucking thing about herself.

Oh, she liked that word.

But something told her she often refrained from using it and now she had to wonder why.

"You and I have known each other since we were babies," Thane said.

"I've been told that but no offense, it's not anything concrete. Tell me about our first date."

Gayle burst out laughing.

Thane raked his fingers through his hair. "That wasn't a date, Mama. We were nine. Not fifteen."

"I don't care," Gayle said. "It was the cutest thing Samantha and I ever saw."

"Samantha." Odessa's heart pounded with the painful memory. "That's my mother, right?"

"Yes, dear." Gayle shimmied to the edge of the seat and took Odessa's hand.

"I can't picture her; I just know that's her name." Odessa searched her empty brain for nuggets of her past. Her history. Her family. She searched every dark corner for anything.

And found nothing but the name. She couldn't even attach it to her father's name. Oh, wait. It started with a *D*. "Does my dad's name start with a *D*? Is it Dav... no, that's not it."

"It will come to you." Gayle took her hand and patted it gently. It was so familiar. So loving. So warm.

An image filled Odessa's mind. Distant and fuzzy at first. It was like a faraway mountain that she drove toward, but it was taking forever. She squinted, trying to draw it closer.

"What is it?" Thane asked.

"Something's forming," she whispered. "Give me a minute."

"Take all the time you need." Thane rested his hand on her thigh. While he gave her great comfort, there was conflict there.

Perhaps that's what came with long history.

She pushed every thought out of her mind and focused only on the forming memory. Only, the more she tried to race toward it, the fuzzier it became.

"I might need help with some details." She squeezed her eyes tight. "Thane and I are walking down a street. It's dark, but I can see the moon in the sky. We have backpacks and a suitcase?" She blinked open her eyes. "That can't be right. Why would two small children be strolling through town with luggage?"

Gayle giggled. "Because you decided to elope. It was adorable. Both your father and Thane's dad followed you. The best part was that you thought you'd make it all the way to the campgrounds for the night."

"We barely made it out of town." Thane smacked his forehead. "I thought I'd try my hand at hitchhiking. Your dad didn't take too kindly to that and intervened."

"How old were we?" she asked.

"I believe Thane had just turned ten and you're four months younger than he is," Gayle said. "The only reason we punished you kids that night was the hitchhiking. Thane knew better than to do something so dangerous."

"I can't say I really remember the entire event." She dropped her head back and sighed. "I can picture the night. Our surroundings. I remember being happy. Laughing. Walking down the street. I can see the details of my backpack, right down to it being from one of those princess movies. And then a sense of dread when our dads pulled—Darryl. That's my father's name." She bolted upright. "And your father's name was Arnold." Tears welled in her eyes. A crushing pain pressed against her chest. It made it difficult for her to fill her lungs with oxygen.

She was all alone in the world.

Her parents were gone. Her body reacted to this revelation as if it was fresh. As if her folks had perished in that car crash moments ago. She suspected it was because she'd put names to a concept and it had become real.

"That's right, dear." Gayle leaned forward, both arms on the bed. "I'm not a doctor, and I don't begin to understand the mind, but you have plucked a few tiny things about your life. Real things. That's good. It's progress. Hold on to that."

"You've always been a really positive person, haven't you?" Odessa said.

"Life isn't always fair. If you spend your life feeling sorry for yourself, you'll never be able to pick yourself up, dust yourself off, and muddle through the little things, much less the really horrible parts of life that are inevitable because tragedy affects everyone." She reached to the side and raised her cane. "I've dealt with health problems. I lost my husband long before I was ready." She set her cane down and waggled a finger toward Thane. "I thought that one over there died twice and I had to nurse him back to health. During all those times, I didn't have the time nor the patience to feel sorry for myself. Life is too short and too precious to sweat any of the stuff."

"I like that." Odessa pulled the bowl of food closer. "I'm going to need a clean fork because I'm not letting this stuff go to waste."

"My mama made you some cookies too." Thane squeezed her leg before easing off the bed and finding the utensil from the floor. He raced off to the bathroom and returned a minute later with a big smile.

"How are you not three hundred pounds?" Odessa took the fork and stabbed a large chunk of lobster and stuffed it in her mouth. It wasn't hot anymore, but that didn't matter. The cheese clung to the sides of the meat and her taste buds went wild with the flavor. She hoped another image would pop into her head, but it didn't.

"If she cooked like that every day, I might be." Thane strolled around to the other side of the bed. "Speaking of which, I better get you home, Mom." He helped his mother out of the recliner.

They seemed to have such a sweet relationship.

And Thane was obviously a mama's boy.

"Haven will stop by in a bit with a new cell phone." Thane looped his arm around Gayle. "It will be all set up, and my number, along with my mom's, Haven's, and Weston's, will already be programmed in it."

"You didn't have to do that." Odessa smiled.

"Oh, yes, he did." Gayle gave him a good elbow to the ribs. "Don't you dare hesitate to call any of us if you need anything."

"I appreciate it." Odessa decided it was best to stop arguing.

"I'll make sure to send Jenna in if I see her." Thane leaned over and kissed her cheek. "I'll see you first thing in the morning."

Odessa continued to nibble on her food as she watched Gayle and Thane disappear. A dense cloud of loneliness loomed in the fluorescent lighting. She focused on the few memories she had and how they made her feel. She replayed them over and over again. Each time she did, they sharpened, growing in focus, expanding in length.

But nothing new filled her brain.

6

Laughter. Lots of it. And drinking. Shots of harsh liquor. Perhaps too much. Followed by more giggling.

She couldn't remember the last time she'd had this much fun.

With her friends.

They were her friends. Or at least that's what she thought, even if this entire thing was as if she were on the outside looking in.

Or perhaps a black-and-white movie. A drive-in.

Whatever. It didn't matter.

She roasted a marshmallow over an open flame while sipping wine out of a red solo cup. Life didn't get any better than that.

Out of nowhere, a constant ringing filled her ears. It

grew louder and louder, muffling out the conversation that she struggled to hear in the first place. She leaned across the campfire but couldn't make out the words.

Her friends waggled their fingers.

They shook their heads. Their faces had expressions of disappointment.

Were they yelling?

She craned her neck, trying to hear the words her friends were saying, but everything was muffled as if she were under water. However, there was no mistaking the daggers being flung from her friends' eyes.

A dark cloud hovered over Odessa. It swirled and twisted, stretching black fingers from the sky, snatching up her friends, leaving her alone.

The fire blew out. The surroundings changed in a flash. She was no longer sitting in front of her tent. No. She was barefoot and running.

But from what?

"Odessa," the wind whispered her name. Or was it a man? She couldn't tell. "You can't hide. I'll find you."

It was cold. It was dark. Only the moon and the stars guided her through the thick brush. Tree limbs smacked her body. Roots lunged from the ground, grabbing her feet and forcing her to fall to her knees.

"I'm coming for you, Odessa. You can run, but you can't

hide," the sinister voice said as a sharp pinprick jolted into her neck.

The world went black.

Odessa gasped and jerked upright. She sucked in a deep breath, blinking. Her chest hurt. She rubbed the side of her neck. It felt as though someone had stuck her with a needle.

She glanced toward the window. The faint glow of the sun beginning to rise filtered through the glass pane. The dream played over in her mind. It was a hodgepodge of images that didn't make sense.

Was it a memory?

A nightmare that had no bearing on her current situation other than she was utterly terrified. Quickly, she gathered her pen and journal and jotted down what she could remember. It wasn't much. She did what Jenna suggested and didn't worry too much about making sense of it. She didn't write in complete sentences. Just jotted down as many details as she could, even though she worried everything was out of sequence.

Setting the notebook aside, she stared at the phone that Thane had bought. Throughout the night, it had given her great comfort, knowing she had a lifeline to the world outside this room. To a person who could connect the dots to her past.

She pulled up the text string with Thane. In the last message he'd sent, he'd told her to do her best to get some sleep, but that he'd leave his cell on in case she needed him. He mentioned that he found her suitcases, but he hadn't said where he'd found them. Only that he'd fill her in on the details when he picked her up in the morning to bring her back to his place.

Her fingers shook as she contemplated sending a message. Outside of Jenna, Anita, and the nice nurses at the hospital, she didn't know who she could trust.

Grant hadn't come back to visit. Nor had he called.

She'd been engaged to him and she thought it was odd that he didn't seem to care, but she couldn't remember anything about their relationship. All she had was the bad vibe that he gave her and that was enough to make her not want anything to do with him in this moment.

Thane, on the other hand, gave her mixed emotions. He was kind and had soft eyes. But she also knew there was something else there. A hint of something negative in their past and that drove her crazy.

Odessa: *Are you awake?*

Thane: *Yes. Is everything okay?*

Did she dare tell him about the dream? Did she wait for Jenna and tell her? Or the police? Haven gave her a warm fuzzy feeling and at the same time projected a badass bitch spirit.

Fuck it.

Odessa: *I had a bad dream. It was about camping.*

Thane: *Did you do what the doctor suggested and put what you can recall in your journal?*

Leave it to him not to badger her about whatever she'd remembered. Why she thought he was sensitive that way, she had no idea.

Odessa: *Yes.*

She didn't know what else to say about that.

Thane: *That's good. Do you want to talk about it? You can call me if you want.*

Odessa: *I'm not sure I want to relive it right now.*

Thane: *I understand. I need to jump in the shower. Then I'm having breakfast with my mama. I'll be at the hospital around ten to bring you home. If you need anything, don't hesitate to call. Okay?*

Odessa: *Do you always call your mom, mama?*

She smiled. Of course he did. A vision of sitting around a dinner table with his mama, his father, him —with his long hair—and her parents, filled her mind. They passed around plates filled with food. They were smiling. Laughing. It brought a tear to her eye.

Thane: *I've been accused of being a mama's boy my whole life. I wear that title with pride. You used to think it was cute.*

Odessa: *I believe I still do.*

Thane: *I'll see you soon. :)*

Odessa set the cell aside, dropped her head back, closed her eyes, and hoped for another memory. Any faint image would do.

But none came.

The door swished open, startling her. She gripped the sheets and blinked. Her heart hammered in the center of her chest. It thumped so hard it hurt. She hated being so scared. But she had no idea if this was normal. Maybe she had anxiety issues. Maybe she'd always been afraid of her own shadow.

Or maybe this was simply because she didn't know shit about her life and her friends were dead.

That thought caught in her throat.

"Good morning," Jenna said. "How was your night?"

"Not great," Odessa admitted. "I'm getting tired of not knowing or understanding my thoughts."

Jenna pointed to the journal. "May I?"

"Of course, but it's a jumbled mess of dreams and thoughts that I can't connect."

"Like I told you yesterday, that will come with time." Jenna flipped through the four pages of notes. "The important thing is that your mind is allowing you to have memories." She set the notebook aside. "That dream must have been terrifying for you."

"It startled me awake. But I'm not sure it's a full memory. Nothing feels like anything other than a snippet here or an old photograph there where I'm not exactly sure of the details. Is that normal?"

"Unfortunately, everyone is different." Jenna leaned against the bed. "I'm going to have my secretary set up a schedule for you. I want to see you a few times a week to start. The first few sessions we'll just talk. If we haven't made much progress, I'd like you to consider hypnosis."

"Does that really work?"

"It can, in some cases."

"I'm willing to do anything," Odessa said.

"That brings me to my next question. Do you

want me to call Grant and tell him what time I'm releasing you?"

"No." The fact that Odessa said that so swiftly and with confidence meant something. She wasn't sure exactly what, but it felt so damn fucking good to belt out that one single word. "Something feels off between him and me, and not just the breakup or the whole bottle-throwing thing. When I think about him, I get a weird vibe through my bones."

"I know it doesn't feel like it, but you control your life. It's your choice where you go. From here on out, you get to decide what you do."

Odessa was tired of hearing that. Not only did she have no idea who she was as a woman, but she didn't know what she did for a living. Nor did she have any idea what kind of financial situation she was in. She was an adult toddler, reliant on everyone. The only way she could reclaim her life was to regain her memories and find out what happened to her friends.

The machine monitoring her heart rate beeped a little faster, in tune with her growing frustration.

"I want to go through my stuff that Thane said the police found, but it's been taken as evidence and he doesn't know when I'll get it back." Odessa sighed. "Do you think I could be blocking out what happened because I did something bad? Is it possible that I could be the reason my friends are dead?"

"My job isn't to make judgments or jump to conclusions about what happened on your camping trip." Jenna held up a finger. "I believe something traumatic happened. Do I personally believe you, the Odessa I know outside of being your doctor, could have hurt your friends? No. I don't think that's possible. Not under normal circumstances."

"That sounds like you think it's possible under a specific set of conditions."

Jenna nodded. "I've been involved in a few forensic cases when it comes to the complexities of the mind. Inherently, you are a good person. I can say that without a doubt, even though we were not friends. We were not close. But most people in this town respect you. Like you. Value you. You're the kind of person the community rallies for, not against."

"But it's possible I snapped." Odessa pulled up the images of the nightmare. They were blurry and flashed across her brain at lightning speed. She tried to slow them down. To pluck out the important ones. Or ones that had to do with what happened to Chrissy and Sylvia, but those raced through her mind even faster. As if her subconscious didn't want her to know the details.

"Those are your words, not mine." Jenna arched a brow. "And it's certainly not a clinical term."

"Have you heard from the therapist I used to see? The one I scheduled an appointment with?" Odessa asked with desperation laced on every syllable.

"I've made a formal request for the files. Unfortunately, Doctor Borden is out of town until this evening. If it's okay with you, I might ask her to join one of our sessions."

"Whatever it takes to get my memories back. Even if I am responsible for what happened, I want to know. This massive void in my head is making me insane."

"I do all my therapy sessions here at the hospital. I generally only see patients two days a week, but I told my secretary to make an exception where you're concerned." Jenna glanced at her watch. "Speaking of which, I've got to get going. I'll start on your discharge papers. I should be able to stop by before you leave this morning."

"I'm sure you're just doing your job, but to me,

it feels like you're going above and beyond. I can't thank you enough for that."

"This is a unique case because two women were murdered. The police are stuck between a rock and a hard place. I understand where they are coming from. They need information. But my first priority is to my patient." Jenna smiled, patting her leg. "Try not to stress. I'll talk to you soon."

Once Jenna was out of the room, Odessa found the remote to the television. She pointed and clicked. The first thing that came up was some woman reporting on the murders.

Wonderful.

She turned up the volume.

"...police have stated that they have interviewed a person of interest, but they are not willing to release the person's name. I've personally spoken to a few hikers who were camping in the area of the murders and they have confirmed that there were three women. Two of those women, Christina Kaymen and Sylvia Wilkerson, are dead. More than one eyewitness has confirmed that the third woman was socialite Odessa Hayes. I've learned that Odessa is no longer engaged to Grant Mercer. We've reached out to Grant but have yet to hear back. We have no other information at this time. We will report any new information to the public as soon as we know something. This is..."

Odessa turned the volume down. Her name was out there for all to judge. Everyone in this town knew more about her life than she did.

Her heart squeezed. Darkness filled her mind. Then a bright light. Then darkness again. It wasn't your typical blackness. It was an eerie void of death, marred with flashes of bright-white lights. Like a strobe pulsating in the distance, barely enough to illuminate wherever this possible memory took her.

The sound of something tearing filled her ears. It was a long rip, followed by a short one.

Stifled cries.

"There you are," a dark, dangerous voice echoed in the recesses of her mind. It was low. It howled like the wind rolling down the waterway, whistling as he rustled the leaves. "You brought this on yourself."

She lifted her gaze. A hazy image leaned over her. It was familiar, but she couldn't make it out.

And then the prick of her skin.

It burned.

Just as quickly as the memory came, the images disappeared.

She jotted it down but decided not to say anything to Thane. They could have that conversation later. Right now, she wanted to focus on something positive and Gayle had said all the photos they left were happy memories. So she reached for the scrapbook and opened it, but her mind didn't flood with childhood memories.

Sure, images flashed. They were two-dimensional and had no context. No meaning.

She tried to remind herself that she was moving forward. That even the tiniest of a memory was still progress. But that didn't ease the anguish in her soul.

7

Thane leaned against the wall and folded his arms across his chest. The smell of antiseptic tickled his nose. He hated hospitals, doctor's offices, and anything having to do with waiting for a medical professional. It wasn't that he didn't trust those caring for Odessa because he did.

But over the course of the last couple of years, he'd spent more time in waiting rooms with his mama while some nurse or doctor told him the same thing.

It was frustrating as bloody fucking hell.

He glanced toward the ceiling and sighed. He hadn't slept well. Tossed and turned most of the night when he wasn't bothering Haven and Weston.

Or texting with Odessa when she messaged him first.

The latter he didn't mind at all.

He found it sweet. Endearing. Especially when she'd recalled a few more memories involving him, even if they were slightly embarrassing.

But waking up to Stacey Burdett's ridiculous news reporting had soured his mood. It was made worse when he'd learned that she'd secured an exclusive interview with fucking Grant for tomorrow morning.

What the fuck was that asshole up to? Whatever it was, it couldn't be good.

"Hey, man," Weston said as he strolled down the hospital corridor decked out in his police uniform. "Did they release her yet?" Weston was a good cop. The best. And an even better man. When Thane had returned to Fallport a few months after his father had died, he learned that Weston and Haven had been stopping by his mother's house on a regular basis. Weston would mow her lawn and fix things around the house. Haven would cook with his mom.

And it wasn't just this couple who helped out.

That had touched Thane in ways he couldn't put into words.

"Nope." Thane shook his head. "Jenna's making me wait out here while she does some neurological test. As I'm sure you've heard, Odessa's been having a few more memories."

"One of the reasons I'm here, but are you sure you want to take this on considering your history?" Weston looped his fingers in his belt buckle and widened his stance.

Typical cop form.

"Where else is she supposed to go?" Thane cocked a brow. "And if you say with Grant, I'll fucking deck you right here."

Weston ran his fingers across his mouth and chin. "You can't deny they were engaged. When all her memories come back, all that history will too."

"Past tense is the operative term there," Thane said. "Besides, Jenna told me Grant hasn't even called to check on her. Not one fucking time. He visited once and that was it. He doesn't care about her. Hell, he doesn't even care about the optics. I'm sure you heard about the stupid interview with Stacey. I can only imagine what he plans on saying during that broadcast."

"I can't say that we're thrilled he's doing that and I've asked him to rethink it. I can't stop him, but I'm hoping he heard me. I'm hoping he understands what he can and can't say." Weston glanced over his shoulder and furrowed his brow. Thane might not have known Weston all that long, but he knew that look. "Haven's discussing it with Stacey and her producer. At least this won't happen until tomorrow, but we don't know what conversations Stacey and Grant have already had."

"What aren't you telling me?" Thane asked.

"This is a complicated case." Weston held up his hand. "I have to look at all the physical and circumstantial evidence. I've interviewed everyone who saw Chrissy, Sylvia, and Odessa at the campgrounds. I've spoken to Leslie Anne as well as others at the car show with Grant."

Thane raked his fingers through his hair. He'd spent his military career looking through a scope. He was a trained sniper. One of the best in the business. He had a quiet patience when it came to his role on his team and he performed his duties without hesitation. He was the man you wanted on your six. He was the overwatch. The one who had his finger on the trigger and would squeeze if he had to. While he was part of the planning of missions, he wasn't a solver of mysteries. He executed missions. He didn't put puzzle pieces together. "What does this have to do with Odessa coming back to my house and me keeping her safe?"

"Grant stopped by the station this morning."

This should be good. "Why?"

"For the record, I shouldn't be telling you anything, especially if she's going to be staying with you."

"Cut the crap, Weston, and get to the point."

"Grant turned over text messages from Odessa from the night of the murders," Weston said. "They are cryptic. Angry. And don't paint her as a stable person."

"That's bullshit. Did you authenticate the messages? Was he willing to turn over his phone?" Thane didn't bother to ask what the messages said because he didn't believe for one second she sent him anything.

"I asked for it and he told me unless I had a court order, he wouldn't do it. That he needed his phone for work and that the printout should be good enough," Weston said. "He stated he only showed them to me because he felt he had to. That he's been concerned about her state of mind for some time now. He went on about how she's had anger issues. That she refused to seek help for her problems. That she's hit him a few times and that while he was even worried she might unleash her wrath on him again, he was willing to give her a place to stay because it was the right thing to do, under the circumstances."

"You've got to be fucking kidding me." Thane pushed from the wall. "That makes no sense at all."

"I read the texts and there is one that I can't ignore."

"Are you going to tell me what it said, or am I going to have to guess?"

Weston blew out a puff of air. "This can't be repeated."

"I know the drill."

"Odessa said if Grant didn't take her back, he'd not only regret it, but she'd do something crazy. Something they wouldn't be able to come back from." Weston lowered his chin. "Before you jump up my ass, I've already gone to a judge for that warrant for his phone. We're still searching for hers. Lincoln and Stormi were able to ping its last location, but it wasn't there. And if I know Lincoln as well as I think I do, he's already doing some shady hacking shit that I don't want to know about, but you're free to ask him."

"I bet Grant has her phone," Thane said under his breath and he would be calling Lincoln and his wife Stormi the first chance he got. They were the most brilliant ethical hackers he'd ever met. Not that he'd known many. "I've known Odessa my entire life. We had our share of struggles before we finally ended our relationship for good. The one thing she never did was give ultimatums. Not once did she tell me it was the Marines or her. Fallport or wherever I was living. It came down to her not taking to military life and me loving it way too much. At the end of the day, we let each other go because we were both too young and selfish."

"Haven mentioned that Odessa wasn't the kind of girl to threaten anyone, but she used to be more vocal. That she was the kind of person to stand up for herself and others. I can't say I've seen her do that lately, and violent? That does seem to be a stretch, but I can't ignore what he put in front of me. I'm a cop. I have to follow every lead."

"Odessa used to have quite a mouth and she could use it to have a good argument with the best of them. But she wasn't violent. She used to like to swear. The word fuck was like a piece of candy to her, but she was never mean. She didn't hit below the belt. She did, however, change when she started dating that asshole. She became docile. The little woman. It was weird. He wanted her to be some high-society piece of arm dressing. I have no idea why he chose her. It makes no sense. She doesn't come from money and the only women he dated, that I knew of, could give him something."

"That might be true, but her parents did have a substantial life insurance policy. And she got about a million for their house."

Thane swallowed. Hard. He hadn't known that. "Where's all that money now?"

"I couldn't answer that question," Weston said. "Odessa stopped being friends with anyone in her old circles. It got worse when she moved in with Grant."

"Tell me something I don't know."

"All right." Weston cocked his head. "Grant's on his way here to take her home."

"Over my fucking dead body."

"I'm a little surprised he didn't beat me here," Weston said. "I had to drop the paperwork off at the courthouse for the warrant for his phone. I did call Jenna. I wanted her to know. Just in case there was an issue between you and him. Please don't make me haul you into county."

"All I can promise is I won't swing first. That would break my mama's heart."

"I guess I can be grateful you're such a mama's boy."

"There's nothing wrong with that." Thane smiled, but it quickly faded. "Motherfucker, here comes that asshole. And he brought Rufus with him. I don't know who I hate more." Luckily, Frick and Frack were stopped at the nurses' station.

"You went to high school with both of them, right?"

"We all played football and lacrosse together. Also graduated the same year. Grant went off to some fancy college and Rufus joined the Army." Thane wiggled his fingers and rolled his shoulders. The last thing Odessa needed was for him to get into it with Grant. But he wasn't about to let her walk out of this hospital with that man. "I need to get to Odessa before he does."

"I don't know how that will work, but Jenna just stepped from Odessa's room." Weston jerked his chin.

Jenna walked briskly down the corridor.

Every muscle in Thane's body tensed and twitched. While he would love to put his fist through Grant's nose, it wouldn't solve anything, except maybe get him tossed from the hospital. No. He couldn't have that. He needed to be prepared to whisk Odessa out of this place and back to his house where he and his mother could take care of her while her memories continued to form.

And the cops figured this bullshit out.

"Good morning, gentlemen." Jenna rubbed the back of her neck. "I was hoping to have a little more time with Thane before that one showed up, if he showed up at all." She grabbed Thane by the arm. "Weston, please see if you can run interference with Grant. I don't want him going in Odessa's room just yet. If at all. Feel free to inform him that she does not want to go home with him. She's made that perfectly clear."

"I might enjoy doing that." Weston nodded.

Thank God for small fucking favors.

Jenna waved to a nurse. "Tell the officer at Odessa's door that no one is to disturb the patient until I return. If anyone balks, instruct the officer that it has to do with some testing." She dragged Thane around the corner, behind a big desk.

"Care to tell me what the hell is going on?" Thane asked.

"Odessa's had a few more memories."

"I know. We've been texting throughout the night and morning. She's told me about the nightmare. About a few other random things regarding that night. She's also had a few other memories about her childhood, but—and these are her words—everything is like a flat black-and-white vintage image."

"It's very frustrating for her," Jenna said. "She told me your knowledge of her life is helpful. But her mind is starting to flood with more memories. She's struggling to categorize them. Most of them are either from when she was a small child through her early twenties or a few from that night. What concerns me is the drug we found in her system and the fact she seems to be remembering what could have been an injection into her skin."

"Shouldn't you be telling this to the cops?"

"I already called Haven and I'm sure she's told her husband." Jenna nodded. "I doubt they would appreciate me telling you, but since you'll be taking care of her, I want to strap you with some information."

"Thanks, Jenna."

She rubbed the back of her neck. "It's possible, because of the amount of alcohol in her system, the way this date rape drug works, and depending on when it was given to her, that she might not ever remember what happened after the injection."

"Which means even if she did witness someone

murder her friends, she might not be able to recall those details," Thane said as a statement, not a question. "What about hypnosis?"

"She's agreed, but I need her to have more of a sense of self. That's where you come in."

"Name it. I'll do anything to help her."

"You're not going to like it." She cocked her head and kept talking. "I want you to come with her to counseling. I want you to be involved in her recovery. Outside of Grant, whom she has too many negative feelings toward, you're the only person she has. I believe you can push her faster into remembering."

"Wait a second." Thane pinched the bridge of his nose. "Just yesterday you wanted to ease her into all this."

"I know. But she's struggling and two women are dead. While Odessa's recovery is my main focus, she's getting herself worked up over it all. She knows she's the key. She wants to open that door no matter the consequences to herself. I need to do it in a safe environment. That means I need your help. Are you willing to do it?"

"If Odessa wants me there, then yeah, I'll come with her." He lowered his chin. "I'll do what I can to help her outside of therapy, but she's in the driver's seat. I will not be a controlling asshole like her ex."

"You're a lot of things, Thane, but controlling is not one of them." She squeezed his biceps. "Now come on. Let's get you to her room. Maybe Weston can make—"

"You can't keep me from seeing her," Grant yelled.

Thane stuck his head around the corner and groaned.

"What the fuck is he doing here?" Grant waggled his finger in Thane's direction.

"Don't start anything," Jenna whispered.

"I never do." But he did finish things. That was always his problem. He inched closer toward Odessa's room.

The officer had positioned himself directly in front of her door. He placed one hand on the butt of his weapon, the other at his side, while his stance widened, and he puffed out his chest.

Thane would think twice about taking down that man without backup.

"Get out of my way." Grant tried to sidestep Weston.

"You need to first lower your voice." Weston continued to block his path. "Odessa is in the middle of some test, so no one is going in her room right now. When those tests are completed, I will be the only one going in to have a second interview."

Nicely played.

Only, that meant he, Grant, and Rufus would be left out here with only the cop at the door. That might not be good.

"And I believe I made it clear that Odessa doesn't want to—"

"How would you know what Odessa wants," Grant interrupted Weston. "Odessa can't even remember who she is. If she's asking to go home with that piece of shit over there, then she's being brainwashed. I demand to see her before she's discharged."

"Maybe you should have considered calling and checking in on her throughout the evening," Thane said. "Or visiting her more than once."

"Fuck off," Grant mumbled. "You don't know shit."

"I will not have that kind of language in my hospital." Jenna stood between Grant and Weston, while Thane hung closer to the uniformed police officer. "I'm sorry, Grant, but Odessa has made her wishes clear. You need to respect them."

"I want to speak with her," Grant said.

Thane's cell vibrated in his back pocket. He pulled it out and stared at the screen.

Odessa: *Tell Jenna I'll speak to him.*

Thane: *That's not necessary.*

Odessa: *It's the only way he'll leave. Let me do this, without you in the room.*

Thane: *I'll tell her.*

He squared his shoulders and inched closer. "She wants to see him." He showed Jenna his cell.

"How on earth would you know that?" Grant glared.

"Doesn't matter. You get your wish," Thane said. "But Rufus stays out here. You go in with Jenna and the rest of us stay out here."

"Fine." Grant lunged forward, bumping into Thane's shoulder.

Fucking jerk.

"And when I come out, Odessa will have realized she made a mistake," Grant said.

Thane curled his fingers around Jenna's biceps. "Do I need to ask Weston to go in there with you?"

"We'll be okay." Jenna smiled. "I know how to handle men like Grant," she whispered. "Don't get yourself in trouble out here."

"I'll behave. I promise." He held Rufus' stare. Back in the day, they'd co-existed well enough.

They had to. Thane was the starting quarterback, and Rufus was his star running back. On the field, they did their jobs. Off the field, they couldn't stand the sight of each other. It had more to do with Grant and the division between the haves and the have-nots.

None of that mattered to Thane, but it mattered to Grant and his groupies.

But what really brothered Grant during those four years of high school was that Thane was the starting QB and Grant wasn't much of a wide receiver. He didn't go on to play college ball.

Not that Rufus or Thane had—but both could have.

A sour subject with Grant.

Thane had always hoped the Army would do Rufus a world of good. He'd been a rich rebel without a cause. His story was cliché. A product of divorce. A kid who had been born with a silver spoon in his mouth. He had everything money could buy.

But he never had his parents' love.

His mother was the whore who ran off with an insurance salesman.

And his dad was a high-powered lawyer who didn't have time to parent, but demanded his kid be the best. When Rufus wasn't, his dad decided it was either the military or he would cut him off.

Rumor had it that eventually his father did pull the purse strings. However, six years into Rufus' military career, his old man passed away. Dropped dead of a massive heart attack.

A widow maker.

Thane truly felt bad for Rufus.

But it didn't soften him. Not one bit.

He struggled to find his way and then came back to Fallport and became Grant's bitch boy.

Rufus casually leaned against the wall. "I heard you're going to be the offensive coordinator for the high school football team next fall."

Thane jerked his head. This was not a conversation he thought he'd ever have with Rufus. "I am."

"That's cool." Rufus nodded. "Did you play at all after high school?"

"My unit in the Marines put together scrimmages, but nothing big." This had to be the weirdest chat Thane ever experienced. "What about you?"

"Not really." Rufus lifted his chin toward the door. "For the record, I don't think it's a good idea if she comes home with him."

"Oh yeah. And why's that?" Thane shifted his

weight. This could be the part in the discussion that tossed him over the edge, forcing him to break his promise to Jenna. Something he didn't want to do.

Rufus closed the gap, standing two paces away. He was an impressive man. Not your typical running back at nearly six foot. He was broad, and currently, Thane figured he was close to two hundred pounds of solid, lean muscle.

Thane was six-four and two forty.

But that didn't mean he could take Rufus.

"I know what you think of me. Hell, there's never been any love lost between the two of us," Rufus said. "Although, I'm not exactly sure why that is."

"I do and it's got a name. Grant Mercer."

Rufus chuckled. "Fair enough. But I'm only here because he's paying me to be. Not for any other reason. I know everyone in this town thinks he owns me because it's my security firm that handles his dealerships and right now, I'm his personal bodyguard."

"Why does he need one?"

"When it comes to Grant, I've learned over the years not to ask too many questions, but it's not because of her; however, that's the spin he'll put on it."

Thane threaded his fingers through his hair and glanced down the corridor. It had been a long while since he spent any significant time with Rufus. He didn't pay much attention to his life. He knew he spent twelve years in the military and then returned to Fallport, creating his security firm, which appeared to be successful.

One of his bigger clients was Grant and his dozen dealerships.

But that was the IT aspect of the business and Leslie Anne ran that internally.

Thane had only been back for a little over a year and he'd seen Grant more times than he cared to admit. However, he'd only seen Rufus a handful of times. But what disturbed him was each time Grant had been at his side.

"What is he going to say about it and why the hell are you telling me?"

"I owe Grant." Rufus arched a brow. "It's a long story and no one knows the details. It's no one's business. But let's just say I'm getting tired of being his lapdog and I'm looking for a way out."

"I'm not that ticket and I sure as shit don't trust you," Thane said. "And you haven't told me anything."

"I've been trying to distance myself from Grant

for the last few years, but it's not been easy. For whatever reason—and I don't know what that reason is—he's pushing this agenda that Odessa has been abusing him." Rufus held up his hand. "He's going to go on television tomorrow and tell that juicy piece of gossip to Stacey."

"Then why does he want to bring her home?"

"I only know so much and I'm only willing to give you so much while we're standing here with him so close. Not to mention you haven't agreed to help me."

"I'm going to need to know why you owe him," Thane said.

"We'll need to have that conversation when we have more time and in private," Rufus said. "Understand that Grant never intended to let Odessa go. I don't believe for one second he's the one who ended it with her. Just last week he forced her event planning business on me for a party I wasn't even going to have. The key here is that Grant wants something. Or needs something, and she's a pawn."

"Let me ask you this." Thane wondered if he was playing with fire, if Rufus would go back to Grant with this conversation, but it was worth the risk. “Do you think Grant could be responsible for what happened to Sylvia and Chrissy?”

“Are you asking me if I think he could have murdered them?” Rufus asked with wide eyes.

Thane nodded.

“Jesus,” Rufus muttered. “Grant’s a lot of things. Shady when it comes to business and he and Leslie Anne have been screwing each other for months, but murder? I don’t know.”

“What about hiring someone?”

Rufus narrowed his stare. “I’m not a killer for hire, if that’s where you’re going with this.”

“We’ve both done and seen shit in the military.” Thane pursed his lips. “People of this town have a certain perception of you. Most of it isn’t good.”

“I’m aware.” Rufus nodded. “Let’s set up a time to chat. I think we can help each other out.”

“How do I know you won’t throw me and Odessa under the bus?”

“Because I’m going to feed you intel as I get it and it’s going to be spot-on,” Rufus said. “And once you hear why I owe him, you’ll understand.” He waved his finger toward the door. “Now let’s go back to pounding our chests, or Grant might think we’ve both gone soft.”

Odessa sucked in a deep breath and let it out slowly. Her mind flowed like a raging river. It was as if she were in a raft, bumping across from one shore to the next, hurling over rocks while she tried to snag branches to slow the flood of memories.

Her first kiss.

Winning the volleyball state championship.

High school graduation.

Watching the bus roll away with Thane on it when he joined the Marines.

The tears when they broke up and her trip to Europe. That had only made her want to get back together.

But it didn't last.

The crushing pain when Thane came home one Christmas with *her*.

Her parents' deaths.

She clutched her chest.

And Grant. That entire relationship flashed before her eyes like the shower scene in *Psycho*. It was brutal. Painful. Horrifying.

Grant's angry words vibrated through the hospital walls. All she needed was to hear Grant's raised voice to revive her life.

Go figure. Had she known that, she would have begged him to visit and then picked a fight.

His voice grated on her nerves like cheese being aggressively shredded on a metal grate, even though it was muffled.

The memories filled her brain like an exploding fire hydrant. There was no shutting it off. No turning down the pressure. It would stop when the last memory was uploaded.

It was strange. The earlier visions were hazy—barely a faint recollection.

These weren't like that at all. But they couldn't be called memories either. They were her life in living color and it rejuvenated—and angered—her.

She texted Thane. She needed to speak with Grant. To see him. To tell him that she was done—with him. It would help her reclaim her life. Her heart pounded in her ears. Fear prickled her skin. She knew what kind of man Grant was. She knew how easily manipulated she could be by him.

But she still needed to lay that hammer down.

Then she'd deal with Thane. It wasn't the same with him because he was a decent and kind person. However, boundaries needed to be made clear. Those memories had smacked her chest too. There was also pain when it came to Thane. Judgment. Anger. Resentment.

But—if she was being honest—there was so much more, and not just coming from Thane. She felt it too.

She choked on a sob. She had no idea what happened to her friends—other than they were dead. Those memories were locked in some dark corner of her brain. Hidden in a cave. Protected by some barrier as if reaching them might destroy her. But she'd find them. She had to. No matter what. She didn't care what she had to do—she needed the truth.

The door squeaked open. Jenna walked in first, followed by Grant. God, she couldn't wait to lay into him. When she'd left her ring… instinctively, she covered her left hand.

No ring.

She'd given it back. But she hadn't done it with gusto. That was about to change. Grant Mercer would see the real Odessa Hayes. Not the weak, scared woman he'd created.

He puffed out his chest and rubbed his temple right near the black eye she supposedly gave him, but that never happened. She remembered exactly what transpired Thursday evening.

However, she couldn't prove it.

It would be her word against his and he was a powerful man in the community.

Her resolve to confront him weakened. The hair on the back of her neck stood on end.

You can run, but you can't hide.

Those were the words she heard in the woods in the dark of night. It was like the wind sang them to her in a familiar timbre. That was the only part of her life that hadn't come back.

Bits and pieces of the night with her girlfriends shuffled around in her brain like a puzzle, but nothing fit. Nothing made sense. There was laughter. Drinking.

And then tension with terse words.

Did someone give her an ultimatum?

"Good morning, Odessa." Grant dared to smile that fake, sweet grin that had most playing out of the palms of his hands. "I hope you slept well." Thankfully, he stood at the end of the bed.

If he had sat on the edge, she might have shoved him off with force.

He held her stare with a crinkled brow, as if to gauge the situation. He could be a calculating man. He was smart. Intimidating. And he almost always got his way. When he didn't, he found the weak spot, exploited it, and made sure he got what he wanted in the end.

He always did.

"I'm surprised to see you," she said behind gritted teeth. One thing she knew about her feelings for Grant was that at this point, she loathed him for what he'd done.

He cocked his head. "I'm here to bring you home."

"I don't want to go with you." In defiance, she folded her arms. He hated that and she knew it.

"I understand how confusing this all must be for you. But I'm sure you will recover faster if you come back to the only home you've known for the last six months." He shifted his gaze toward Jenna. "Don't you agree, Doctor?"

"I'm sorry, but this is her decision." Jenna leaned against the side of the bed, holding her hand. "What's important is how she feels about her recovery, and wherever she wants to go, I'll support."

It was nice to have someone in her corner.

Odessa wondered what Jenna was going to say when she found out that Odessa remembered most events in her life.

"Listen, you're the doctor and I agree with you

that Odessa should feel a certain way, but I don't think sending her home with someone who is essentially a stranger to her isn't what's best," Grant said. "We might have fought and needed a break, but I'm her fiancé. She barely knows Thane anymore. They aren't friends and she's made it perfectly clear to him over the last few months that she doesn't appreciate his advances." He leaned over and squeezed her ankle.

She cringed.

"You've told him that so many times. I wish you could remember the frustration he's caused you. The fights it's caused us," Grant said.

That was absolutely not true and she wanted to correct Grant, but something told her it was best if he didn't know she had her memories back. It wasn't the right time to confront him with anything. The only thing she needed to do was make sure she didn't go anywhere with him, ever.

"Whether that's true or not, I do not wish to go home with you." She lifted her chin. "That's final and I need you to respect that."

"Come on, sweetheart." He inched around to the side of the bed and reached for her hand.

She jerked it away.

"No," she said, shaking her head. "I'd like you to leave now."

"Honey, I know you're scared. I get it. But there are things about Thane you—"

"Excuse me," Jenna said. "It's important that we don't taint the process and this is putting ideas in her head."

Grant arched a brow. "And he's not—you're not—putting… never mind." He shifted his gaze. "I'm not going to push this right now, but when you change your mind, I'll be here for you. I'm always here for you." He tapped the side of his head, near the bruise. "No matter what happens." He leaned closer. "Or what you've done. I always take care of you."

She swallowed. Hard.

He strolled out the door. "Come on, Rufus. I've got work to do," he said with authority.

Thane ducked his head inside. "Everything—"

"I need a moment with Jenna." Odessa rubbed her temples.

"Okay. I'll be right out here." Thane gently tugged the door closed.

Odessa sat up taller. "I remember. Almost everything. I remember."

"I got that impression." Jenna folded her arms.

"What I want to know is why didn't you tell Grant? Why did you kick Thane out? And should I be asking the police to come in?"

"Last question first." Odessa sighed. "I don't remember what happened to my friends. That night is a blur. I was drunk. I do remember fighting with my friends. But it's like I blacked out."

"You're going to need to make a statement."

"And I will." Odessa nodded. "I had every intention of telling Grant off. I did not give him that black eye. That I remember. But something tells me it was best he does not know I remember anything. I dumped him. But I don't know why he's chosen to lie about it."

"I don't know, but these are all things you need to discuss with the police."

"Again, agreed. But now I have something I want to discuss with you." She narrowed her stare, reeling in her frustration. Her entire world landed in the pit of her stomach. Everyone was suspect. Not in the murder of her friends. She hadn't a clue about that. She couldn't fathom who would want to kill them. Or for what reason. However, whoever did it left one person alive, which meant she was still in danger.

Grant was a lot of things, but a protector, he

was not. Rufus might have a stable of bodyguards, but she did want that man guarding her? No, she'd take her chances with Thane. At least she knew what she was in for when it came to him.

However, that didn't change the fact that she felt manipulated by every person who had walked into this hospital room, including her doctor.

"In the last twenty-four hours we chatted—in passing—about the fact that I used to date Thane. That he took you out a couple of times. But you neglected to tell me that you hate me."

"Hate is a strong word and it's not true."

Thane wanted her to have her voice back. Well, maybe this was what he meant. "Really? Then explain to me why a few months ago, when I'd broken up with Grant for a couple of weeks, and you saw me out with Thane, you got in my face and told me that I either needed to commit to him or release him, but that I couldn't have it both ways."

Jenna opened her mouth, but Odessa just kept talking. She was going to get this out, especially when she hadn't the balls to do it when it happened.

"A few short weeks later, I saw you again. This time I was with Grant. You had the nerve to corner me in the bathroom. You called me a coward. Told me I didn't deserve a man like Thane. You told me to stay away from him. That I was causing him psychological harm. What gives you the right to say that shit to me?"

Jenna turned, pulled up a chair, and planted her ass in it. She sighed. "I'm sorry. I shouldn't have said it."

"Then why did you?"

"Because at the time, I thought I cared about Thane a certain way." Jenna arched a brow. "However, he and I have jack shit in common. I took out my hurt feelings on you and for that I am sorry. Anything else?"

"Yeah." This was not exactly how Odessa expected this to go down, but it felt damn fucking good to get it off her chest.

Finally.

She'd held it so close to the cuff for months. Like she did everything else, because Grant controlled her world.

"Wasn't it a conflict of interest to take me on as a patient?"

"I don't believe so," Jenna said. "I have not tried to control the outcome of your memory recovery process. I've only tried to help you regain them. I also don't have any feelings for Thane romantically. I do consider him sort of a friend, in a weird way."

"I have one last question," Odessa said. "Do you believe, as your patient, that I'm making the right decision about where I will stay? Or could I get a hotel?"

"I would not recommend staying alone." Jenna pushed to a standing position. "You need support and Thane and his mother used to be that for you. I do believe they are a good choice. I also think you should stay away from Grant."

"That, we both agree on." Odessa sighed. "You can send Thane in and get Haven or Weston back down here. I might as well get that statement over with."

"I bet Weston is still out in the hallway." Jenna took her hand. "I'm on your side. Remember that."

Odessa actually believed that.

8

Thane planted his hands on his hips and stared out the big picture window. A million and one things raced through his brain. Not a single one was good. Heat coursed through his veins. He understood the rage he felt toward Grant.

That was easy.

But the rest of it? He had no idea where to direct it.

He shouldn't be mad at Odessa, and frankly, he wasn't. She hadn't done anything wrong. He probably would have done the same thing if he were in her shoes.

There were simply too many questions with not enough answers.

But it was the cryptic note from Rufus left on his

mother's front porch that sent him down a dark and dangerous path.

Thane was a lot of things. He'd been a trained killer for the government. He'd been sent on numerous unsanctioned black ops where if the shit went sideways, his own superiors might have turned against him because they couldn't afford to admit what the mission had really been.

He'd done things in his past that he wasn't particularly proud of, but being a sniper wasn't one of them. His career, while colorful, was something he could hang his hat on. It wasn't about the medals he'd been given. He didn't care about any of that. It had been about being a part of something bigger than himself. About serving his country. About giving back to his community.

And finally, he wanted his parents to be able to puff out their chests, hold their heads high, and tell their friends their boy was a good egg.

Even if he'd done some unspeakable things.

Currently, his mother would smack him upside the back of his head with her cane because of the thoughts he had between wanting to strangle Rufus, punch Grant… and then there was Odessa.

He let out a long breath, tapping his finger against his chest. God, how he loved that woman.

He wouldn't even try to deny it—at least not to himself.

"Hey, Ma?" He turned. "I'm going for a walk. I need to clear my head."

"Wait." His mother hobbled from the kitchen. "You can't just leave. What about Odessa?"

"She's taking a bath. It will be a good half hour before she comes down and it's not like you don't have lots to talk about." He leaned over and kissed his mother's cheek. "Just remember, no one can know she has her memory back."

"You've made that very clear." She reached up and pinched his cheek. "You're also scaring me by having your buddies take turns hanging out down the street."

"Someone murdered two girls and may have tried to kill Odessa." He arched a brow. "I wanted to take her somewhere else, but you threatened me."

"I did not. I just made it clear that poor girl needs family. We're family."

"Then why are you so concerned about being alone with her?" He arched a brow.

"Her anger is bouncing off the walls like silly putty. I'm afraid it's going to smack me right between the eyes." His mom pointed to the bridge of her nose. "I know that girl when she gets like this. She's like a dog with a bone. She won't rest until she finds the answers she wants."

"Unfortunately, those answers aren't going to come easy and there's only one other person who can tell her what she wants to know." He pressed his hands on his mom's shoulders. "And that's a person we don't want to invite into the fold."

His mama shivered.

"I'll be back shortly. I've got my cell. Call if you need me." He headed toward the back door. Quickly, he shot off a text to Jett, a fellow park ranger, who was currently keeping watch. He was taking a calculated risk by bringing in his team, but he trusted them.

He didn't trust Rufus. However, he did want to hear him out.

Jett: *You want backup?*

Thane: *Nope. Just keep an eye. Thanks.*

Thane strolled down the street. His mother lived in a small neighborhood just outside of town. Only about twenty houses. It had its own pool and playground. It was cozy and quiet.

The park was dark, since technically it was closed. He made his way across the basketball court to the benches where Rufus was already waiting.

"I wasn't sure if you were going to show up." Rufus crossed his legs, stretching out both arms on the back of the bench.

"What is so important that we had to meet in the dark?" Thane sat on the far side of the bench. Never in his life had he considered Rufus a friend. But at one point they had been teammates. They trusted each other on the field. They were a good pair. Quarterback and running back. They took the team to a state championship—twice. Whatever their differences were off the field, they left them there once the ball had been kicked.

Hell, sometimes they even found themselves laughing on the sidelines or in the locker room. But once Grant got involved, all bets were off.

"I'm supposed to be looking for an opportunity to break into your house and bug it." Rufus shifted, leaning forward, resting his forearms on his knees. "I'll go back to Grant and tell him that you've got the cops, some buddies, and your mom constantly hanging around and that it was too risky. But he'll send someone else. He's got a few men from my payroll that he'll be able to get to break in here in the middle of the night or when you and Odessa are out. I'd hate that for your mom. She's a sweet lady."

Thane ran his hand across his mouth. "Why do you care?"

"I'm tired of Grant holding two things over my head." Rufus waggled his fingers. "And while you and me have never been friends, we're cut from the same cloth."

"I wouldn't go that far... I mean with the whole cloth statement."

"I beg to differ." Rufus leaned back. "We both have certain traits. Back in the day, we were both able to compartmentalize our chest-pounding, keeping it to a minimum."

"I'll give you that." Thane nodded.

"We also had jobs in the military that required us to do certain things that weren't for the faint of heart."

"Where are you going with this?" Thane asked, not wanting to play a game of twenty questions.

"I've never corrected anyone regarding what happened between me and my dad," Rufus said. "People in this town like to gossip and they wanted to believe that because I was rough around the edges, my dad would always cut me off." He shrugged. "But he didn't. I walked away. I didn't want his money."

"But you got it when he died."

"Yeah, that shocked me. I think it shocked Grant too," Rufus said. "At the time of my father's death, he and I weren't speaking. But I wasn't speaking to Grant either."

Thane jerked his head back. "Now that does surprise me. Grant and your dad were always so close. Because of that, I believed—as everyone else—that even though your dad treated you like shit, you put up with it because you wanted his money."

"I was over my old man, this town, and Grant. I had a career that I could be proud of, I was making my own money, though not very much, and I had a girl who made me happy. My dad's money wasn't even on my radar. To me, that inheritance would have been—and was—a bit of a death sentence."

"I don't understand. What happened?"

"It wasn't one thing, but a chain of events." Rufus blew out a puff of air and leaned back. "I seriously thought that my dad—to spite me—would leave his fortune to Grant. That honestly would have made my day and we wouldn't be sitting here right now having this conversation. As a matter of fact, you and I might even be friends."

"I'm not sure I'd go that far." Thane chuckled. "We kind of hated each other in high school."

"I never hated you. I was an angry little shit

with daddy and mommy issues. Grant had been my best friend since grade school. He had my father's ear. More importantly, he had my father's love. Something I desperately wanted back then. The Army taught me all I needed was my self-respect. I've lost that and I want to gain it back. But in order to do that, I need to tell you a little story."

"No offense, man, but I'm not sure I will believe anything that comes out of your mouth."

"That's fair, but I'd like you to hear me out." Rufus glanced toward the sky. "Because my dad left me everything, I had to come back and bury him. It was my first time seeing or speaking to Grant in a few years. I didn't want to do jack shit for the old man, but Grant had different plans. He worshipped my dad. He wanted to do this grand memorial. It made me sick to my stomach, but I didn't have any fight in me, and Yolanda, my girlfriend, she told me to let Grant have it. Hell, she told me to give him the money if it meant putting all this bullshit behind me."

"Did you?"

"Fuck no," Rufus said. "One thing I know about Grant is he's a greedy bastard. He approached me with a business proposition and I entertained it for a hot minute. But I was still in the

Army and I blew him off. Went home to find my house had been robbed and my girlfriend raped and murdered."

"Jesus Christ," Thane mumbled. "I'm so sorry."

"It was the worst day of my fucking life," Rufus said. "But, man, Grant showed up at my doorstep. He was there for me when I needed a friend the most." Rufus ran a hand across his face. "I was in a bad place. I had done something most men wouldn't come back from." He held Thane's gaze with the steely eye of a sniper.

"What did you do?"

"Exactly what you think I did." Rufus swiped at his eyes. "Revenge killing isn't the same as killing for God and Country. When we pull that trigger because we're making the world safe from terrorists. Killing leaders who threaten freedom, we have purpose. We can justify our actions. Sure, I had reasons for strangling the life out of that man, but I didn't let our justice system, the very system that I took an oath to defend when I joined the Army, work. I took matters quite literally into my own hands."

"What does this have to do with Grant and the situation we are in right now?"

"As much as I knew the world was a better place

without that asshole, I was struggling to live with the guilt. If you thought I was a rebel without a cause back in high school, I was ten times worse during this time. I was fucking up left and right and I was facing disciplinary action in the military. Grant made it his life's mission to save my sorry ass. He talked me into leaving the military. He helped bury evidence that would prove I killed that man. That it was premeditated and in cold blood. That fucker even has a recording of me confessing the crime." Rufus arched a brow.

"Are you trying to tell me that Grant has been blackmailing you all these years?"

"No. Not at first. Grant doesn't work that way. He's more subtle than that." Rufus leaned back, stretching out his legs. "Once I was out of the Army, I came back to Fallport. Not so much because I wanted to, but because I didn't know where else to go. I still thought my life was over. I was constantly looking over my shoulder, waiting for the cops to knock on my door. But they never did. Grant took care of everything and I let him. About six months after I returned, I started my security business—with Grant's help. At first, he was hands-off. He's always good that way. Acting as if he cares. As if he's on your side and only wants what's best.

But before I knew it, he had his grubby little greedy fingers in every aspect of my business and I became his bitch boy." Rufus held up his hand. "I don't want to go to prison. I know what I did was wrong, no matter how I try to justify it, but deep down, I'm not a bad man."

"Can I ask you a difficult question?" Thane wasn't sure what to do with this intel. It was a lot to take in. He shouldn't be surprised by what Rufus told him about Grant, but Thane was shocked by the entire tale.

"I just told you something that only one other person knows. You could fuck me over good. So, yeah, you can ask me anything."

"Did you actually plan that man's murder? And I'm not talking about thinking about what it would be like if he were dead, because that's a normal reaction to have when someone you love is killed."

"You know, I've thought a lot about that but I'm not sure it matters."

"Why do you say that?"

"Because of that audio recording. He has me admitting it. He has me saying I went to that man's house intending to kill him," Rufus said with real emotion laced to every word. "I was blinded by rage and brutal grief. It's hard to sort through my state of mind. I wanted him to suffer. I wanted him to pay for what he did to my precious Yolanda."

"I'm not cop. Or lawyer for that matter, but I do believe your intent matters in this case. Crimes of passion are a thing."

"Maybe so. But Grant has me to the wall and he's getting more ballsy. If I don't do what he wants, not only will he find someone else to do it, but he'll turn me in and turn over what he has," Rufus said. "Like I said, I don't want to go to prison."

"So, what do you want from me? What do you think I can do for you?"

"I'm not sure you can do anything for me." Rufus sighed. "I told you what Grant expects me to do and I also told you that I'm not going to bug your house. At least not tonight. But Grant won't stop until he gets what he wants. If I don't do it, he'll get someone else. Someone more loyal than me."

"Or he'll do it himself."

"Doubtful. It's rare he does his own dirty work," Rufus said. "He's pretty good at keeping his hands clean."

"Why does he want to bug my home?"

"You really have to ask?"

"Yeah, because while you don't believe he's

capable of murder, I do." Thane cocked his head. "We did for our country. You were pushed to it because someone took the love of your life from you. But Grant? Does he even have any compassion? Empathy? Come on, man. Be honest about that."

Rufus snorted. "Grant's an arrogant prick. But he's also a pussy. Why do you think he walks around with me or someone from my company? He's scared of his own fucking shadow. He was all talk back in the day. He'd shoot his mouth off, but he always needed my fists to stand up for him. He needs muscle to do what he does."

"Or he's a master manipulator and he's playing us all and has been for years," Thane said. "Tell me this, why does he want to bug my house? What does he think he's going to find out?"

"I don't ask too many questions. That pisses him off. He wants blind loyalty and since I've been poking the bear, he's been reminding me a little too much about how he could destroy my life. But my best guess is to learn when Odessa comes into her memories. To him, she's his property and he doesn't like it when people walk out on him."

"Did he take all her money?"

"I can't be completely positive about that, but

yeah, I believe so. I mean, he's managed to find ways to get lots of mine," Rufus said. "In the beginning, I didn't care because I looked at my dad's money as a burden. But he's got a big hold on my company."

"Explain that to me."

"Grant's good at swooping in and helping someone pick up the pieces of their life. He helped set everything up for my firm. He did all the grunt work. What I didn't know at the time was he's my partner. I can't do shit without his approval. At first, he stayed out of it. But eventually, he started flexing his muscles. Inserting his ideas into what I thought was my business."

"What kind of decisions has he made that you wouldn't have?" Thane rubbed his temple, wondering how many people—businesses—Grant's fingers were in. He inherited his father's dealerships. He was partners with Rufus. There was Odessa's event planning business. Was there anyone else? And why?

"Besides being a top marksman and recon skills, I learned a lot of things in the military. Security detail and security technology among them," Rufus said. "I always planned on starting a business like this when I left the military. Set up commercial security, contract bodyguard for a certain type of clientele. It's a great gig. I do love it. But Grant has started to hire some shady men. Guys that have never put men and mission first." Rufus arched both brows and lowered his chin. "And in that order. These are the kind of guys who think in terms of money and power and they will kill to get it."

"That means Grant could have hired someone—"

"I didn't say that," Rufus said. "What you have to understand about Grant is his family didn't have the kind of money they pretended to have when we were kids, but even he didn't know until we graduated. It was a huge blow to his ego. His dad was in debt up to his eyeballs and was about to lose everything. My father paid for Grant's fancy college education and bailed out his old man when he nearly lost the dealerships." Rufus rubbed his nose. "Grant started doing a lot of coke back then and he still does. And while he's a greedy fucking asshole, I don't believe he would ever kill anyone or hire someone to do it for him. Now, would he rob you? Take all your money and not think twice? Yeah. That he'd do."

"I don't know why you—or anyone—feels like

they need to defend him after all the shit he's done to you," Thane said. "Have you ever thought about going to Haven or Weston with your situation?"

"Are you fucking crazy? Weston can't stand me and honestly, I don't blame the man. I play my role and keep my distance from people in this town. I've been looking for a way out, not just with Grant, but in general." Rufus waved his hand. "And when it comes to Haven, well, I know what she went through and she might be a little more reasonable, but still, she's a fucking cop. And a good one. She'll slap those cuffs on me so fast I won't have time to find a high-priced attorney."

"I don't believe that." Thane stood and stretched. "How well do you know Lincoln and Stormi?"

"Not well."

"They're good people. Smarter than anyone I know. Let me ask them to look into not only the case file on what happened to your girlfriend, but maybe they can hack into Grant's computer or phone and find something that can release you."

Rufus jumped to his feet. "That would be unethical for ethical hackers." He laughed. "And something tells me you're already having them do that."

"I might be." Thane pointed toward the entrance of the park. "But I'm also going to allow you to bug my house when I take Odessa and my mom out for ice cream tonight."

"Why the fuck would you do that?"

"Because I want to feed some bullshit to Grant. Once I've done that, Lincoln will come in and do a sweep, because I will have discussed that. So it won't feel like a setup."

"I don't know. Grant's smarter than you're giving him credit for."

"I've already called Lincoln, asking him to come over later so I can talk to him about some things. To ask him to help me do a sweep. Considering I'm a paranoid motherfucker, that won't be a stretch."

"All right. I guess I'm planting a couple of bugs."

"I'll text you—"

"No. Don't contact me at all. I have a feeling Grant's put something on my phone. I'll leave you a note where the listening devices are inside the house. I'll find a way to be in touch later."

"Why don't you contact Lincoln and let him look at your phone."

"Maybe." Rufus held out his hand. "Thanks for not only taking the time, but also believing me."

"If you fuck me over, I will come for you." Thane took the man's hand and squeezed.

"I wouldn't expect anything less." Rufus stuffed his hands in his pockets and strolled down the path as if he didn't have a care in the world.

Thane blew out a puff of air.

It was going to be one long fucking night.

9

"You want me to lie?" Odessa dropped her spoon into her ice cream dish and stared at Thane. Her memories might have flooded her mind like a tidal wave smashing against the shore and curling its massive wave down over the beach. But there were some gaps. Lapses in time and space. She'd see something or hear something, and the blanks would fill in. She hoped that would happen soon with the deaths of her friends.

Jenna told her she had to be patient. That if she tried to force it, they wouldn't come. Or she could have false memories. Odessa didn't want that.

She also didn't want to sit in Thane's house,

have a fake conversation, and lie right through her fucking teeth. "You hate liars." She lowered her chin and glared. "You've always preferred the truth to even a white lie."

"You're exaggerating and this is different than you trying to make me feel better when I had to cut off all my hair." He ran his fingers across the top of his head. "However, I can't imagine growing it back now."

"Yeah, I don't think it would be a good look on you. It would age you and make you look like a fool trying to be cool." She sat up taller and smiled. "How's that for a dose of honesty."

"Much appreciated." He shook his head and chuckled. "You know this isn't the same thing."

She absolutely understood that. But it didn't change the fact she would rather Grant think she was still clueless. It made her life easier. At least until they figured out what happened to poor Chrissy and Sylvia.

God, she couldn't believe they were gone. Or that she might have seen what happened and couldn't remember. Tears burned the corner of Odessa's eyes. Ever since her memories returned, she could barely keep the tears at bay. They came in hot. And fast. Her eyes felt like sandpaper. Thane had drawn a nice hot bath for her and she soaked in it until the water turned to ice. She cried until there were no tears left, and then she sobbed some more.

But nothing could ease the pain in her soul.

"I get the difference, but I don't have to like it." Odessa picked up her spoon, filled it with ice cream, chocolate, and caramel syrup, and plopped it in her mouth. "I don't know why we're trusting Rufus. He's Grant's lapdog. Does whatever he says, whenever he says."

"I believe that's changed. And you told me on the walk over here that the last few months, Rufus hasn't been around as much. Both you and Rufus mentioned this guy Heath Fender. He gives you a bad vibe and Rufus says he's a loose cannon. That he was given a less than honorable discharge from the military. I've got Lincoln looking into that, among other things."

Odessa shoved her ice cream across the table, leaned back, and folded her arms. Jenna had told her to categorize her memories. To mentally put her first eight years in one set of folders and file them away. Then put everything up to when her parents died into another filing cabinet, but not to lock them away. Keep the drawers slightly open and ready when she needed to draw on those memories either for comfort or something else.

The rest, she needed to leave open and at the ready. However, they needed to be organized, and Odessa was still working on that. Her mind was still a kaleidoscope of images smashing into each other while she tried to pluck out the meaning of her life. "I don't really know Heath. I've only met him a couple of times." She tried to pull up those memories. They were few and far between, but something prickled her skin. There was something she was forgetting, but she couldn't figure out what that was. "I understand what you're trying to do and appreciate it. But you're asking me to lie about something really big and because I can't remember, it feels even worse."

Thane reached across the table and took her hand. "I'm asking you to be vague. I don't want you to come out and accuse him of doing something he didn't. But I want him to believe you know more than you do. If he comes after us more than the listening devices in my home, then we'll know we're onto something. If he doesn't, then you can enjoy telling me I was wrong for the rest of my life."

"I don't get why I'm being banished to my cousin's house," Gayle said, breaking her silence.

She hadn't said anything most of the evening. However, she did smack Thane in the shin with her cane when he'd dropped the news. "Tonight. As in twenty minutes from now, Lynn is picking me up at this stupid ice cream shop, I can't believe I don't get a say in this. I should really hurt you with this cane."

"If flying wasn't too hard on you, I'd put you on a plane to California." Thane lowered his chin. "Asher can't come out here right now and trust me, I asked."

"Your brother and his family will be here for a month this summer. He does what he can."

"Ma, I'm not judging Asher and his life decisions. He has a wife, two kids, and a massive winery that needs his attention. He's a good man. A good brother. And a better son. He'd be on the next plane if I told him I had to have him at my side." Thane wiped his mouth and tossed his napkin on the table. He and his older brother didn't always see eye to eye on things. There was a ten-year difference and sometimes Asher pulled the older, wiser brother to the point that Thane tuned him out. Odessa had seen that firsthand.

Whether Thane wanted to admit it or not, he'd felt abandoned when Asher went to college. And not just any university. Asher had the nerve to move to the West Coast and he never came home. Nope. He fell in love and got married at the ripe old age of twenty-two.

Poor Thane had only been twelve and he thought he lost his best friend. That's when he and Asher slowly grew apart.

However, in the last few years, Odessa had learned that Thane and Asher had grown close. Real close. That age gap seemed to have disappeared.

She suspected that had a lot to do with their mother and her illness. And then their father's death.

"But we don't know who killed Chrissy and Sylvia and I need to know if Grant had anything to do with it. Until we figure all that out, I need to know you're safe. It's temporary and you and Lynn always have a good time when you visit."

Gayle leaned forward, resting her arms on the table. She smiled that sweet, genuine smile that made everyone in her presence feel warm and fuzzy. "I know all you're trying to do is take care of me. To do right by your mama." She patted Thane's hand. "You've always done your best to please your dad and me, to make us proud, and you've done that in spades. I have no problem going to Lynn's house for a couple of days while you deal with this situation. It's how you manhandled it. I hated it when your father did that." She cocked her head and narrowed her stare.

Oh, Odessa remembered that look. Gayle gave it right before she was about to lay down the hammer and ground Thane for a week.

"You have always been more like your father. You're the spitting image of him and you have his quiet resolve." Gayle lifted her finger and wiggled it when Thane tried to open his mouth and speak. "Asher is more like me. He's quick to speak his mind. Maybe too quick. He and I say what we think exactly when we think it, whereas you took on your father's trait of letting it settle into your gut. Sometimes that's a wonderful trait because you're logical and not emotional. But other times—because things fester—they get twisted. They eat at your insides like acid and that logic turns into a fireball of emotion."

"Ma, do you have a point in this ramble?" Thane asked.

"I do." Gayle nodded. "Right now, you're in that weird bubble between logic and irrational emotions. I know this because whenever you've wanted me to do something you're not sure I'll be on board with, you sit me down and have a normal conversation. What you did tonight was what your father used to do when he was afraid his work with the US Marshal Service would spill over into our nice cozy family life. I'm not a child. I understood that what your father did could be dangerous. I never once asked him not to do it and I'm damn grateful that's not what killed him." She lifted her hand. "But I hated it when he didn't speak to me like his partner and I don't like it when you speak to me like a child. I'm your mother. And I'm a person. I demand to be treated that way. So, next time, you will tell me what's going on and I will agree to go see my cousin. Got it?"

Odessa covered her mouth, trying to stifle a full-on belly laugh. She sat there, staring at Gayle during that speech. And it was a damn good speech. It reminded Odessa of so many from the past. Like the time Thane's father had been gone for a month on a special project. It was Christmastime and Gayle had decided to climb up on a ladder and hang the lights. Thane was pissed. He told her he'd do it when he got home. But he only had four days leave from the Marines and the first night he had every intention of spending it with Odessa.

When he got to his mom's house and found her on the ladder, he had some choice words. But the best part was he'd climbed halfway up, snagged her right off the wood plank, and plopped her on the Adirondack chair as if she were weightless.

Odessa understood his concern, because of her disease. But Gayle was right. He could be an ogre. Controlling, but not manipulative. Thane was definitely a straight shooter and when it came to his mama, his concern for her well-being outweighed his good judgment.

"What the hell is so funny?" Thane asked, glaring, although the right corner of his mouth twitched, as if he wanted to smile but couldn't bring himself to do it because that meant he had to admit his mama was right.

Another interesting trait about Thane that tickled Odessa's fond memories. Thane was the kind of man who had no problem admitting he was wrong in most cases. But this was the kind of situation he wouldn't bow down to because he was right about how, for the time being, it was best for Gayle to go visit her cousin.

But he was dead wrong for how he handled it.

"You." She lifted her foot and pushed his gently

under the table. It was something she would have done in the past.

When they were together.

But it felt genuine in the moment.

"This." She waved her hand. "Gayle. The whole thing. Nothing's changed. At least between the two of you. You're having the same argument you've always had." Her parents would be so disappointed in how her life turned out and not just because she'd lost the insurance money and sold the family home.

But Odessa had lost herself.

A guttural sob got caught in her throat. She swallowed. Hard. Her entire world was upside down. She didn't know what was worse.

Not remembering her entire life.

Or remembering and realizing how she'd fucked it all up.

And knowing two of her friends—her only friends—were gone and it was her fault.

Her laughter turned into a sloppy cry as a couple of tears dribbled down her cheeks.

Thane stood, made his way around the table, and sat next to her, wrapping his arms around her shaking body. "What's wrong?"

"I don't know. One second I'm back in high

school and the next, I'm remembering my friends are dead," she choked out. Images of her running through the dark woods. Running from something… or someone. The wind howled. It called to her. *Odessa, you can't hide from me.* More flashes of that night blinked in front of her eyes. It was like lightning illuminating the world during a blackout, giving you a glimpse into what was out there, but only for a second. It wasn't enough time for you to really see much of anything. To know if what was in front of you was dangerous or safe. But deep down, she knew her life hung in the balance. That someone was out there—chasing her—and they wouldn't stop until they caught her.

She rubbed her ring finger. "I know I gave Grant the ring back. How did it end up—"

Thane gently pressed his finger over her lips. "I gave you that information in confidence. Weston would have me behind bars for that one, so let's not discuss it out in public," he whispered. "Nor will that be something we mention once we're home. We need to stick to the script. Can you do that?"

Odessa nodded.

"Thane," Gayle said. "I hate to interrupt at a time like this, but Lynn just pulled up. We should get my things from your truck."

"I told Lynn to meet us in the parking lot." Thane kissed Odessa's temple. His lips were soft. Warm. They sizzled against her skin, sending shock waves to the rest of her body.

It wasn't a sexual kiss. The only meaning behind it was comfort. But it reminded her of so many other things, like… she jerked her head back.

Huh. That was a memory that hadn't flooded her mind right away.

Interesting. It was like she'd tucked that indiscretion in a safe and threw away the key. The guilt she felt at the time bubbled to the surface, only to be squashed down by the harsh reality for the reason she'd left Grant the first time.

And the dumbass reason she'd taken him back.

What a fool she'd been.

That was only compounded by the fact that she could clear as day hear Thane whisper, *I love you. I will always love you,* in her ear that fateful night about seven months ago. He'd been so kind. So sweet.

Five days later, she told him she was going back to Grant. The look on Thane's face had nearly destroyed Odessa. It broke her heart—destroyed her soul.

But what was she supposed to do?

Grant had tricked her into selling her family

home and Grant had a firm foothold on her money, which she now knew he'd slowly stolen from her, like he stole everything.

Thane helped her then his mother to their feet. He took his mom by the elbow and laced his fingers through Odessa's. "Since I promised both you ladies I'd be open and honest, you should know that Weston and Haven texted me right before we sat down." He guided them down the corner and into the parking lot, where there weren't any people.

At least not that Odessa could see.

"What did they have to say?" Gayle asked.

"Some of it's not good," Thane said. "Grant's really going for the Odessa being a violent person angle."

"That's bullshit. I never threw a bottle at him."

"It's more than that." Thane squeezed her hand. "It's about those text messages and other lies Grant is spewing. But the good news is the judge gave Weston the warrant for Grant's phone, tablets, and computer." He paused near Thane's vehicle. "Weston also mentioned he's got some other things going on related to the case. He wouldn't go into detail, but he says some things are happening."

"I don't like the sound of that." His mom took the suitcase Thane handed her and tugged on the handle. "I assume there is some kind of protection detail on me and Lynn."

"I put together a rotation between some of the guys at search and rescue and my buddies at Parks and Recreation. I'll send you the schedule so you're not surprised." He leaned over and kissed his mother's cheek. "Want me to roll this bag—"

"I'm perfectly capable of doing that." Gayle patted the side of his face. "You make sure you take good care of Odessa. There's a bunch of leftovers labeled in the fridge and fresh cookies in the cookie jar."

"Thanks, Mama. I love you. Have a great time with Cousin Lynn."

Odessa stood—holding Thane's hand—and watched as his mother, slightly hunched over, tugged her suitcase on wheels across the parking lot. Lynn raced across the pavement and hugged Gayle as if they hadn't just seen each other a few weeks ago.

Huh. Odessa knew that.

She knew a lot of things.

"Grant has been having an affair with Leslie Anne for months." Odessa grabbed Thane by the shoulders. "I don't have the kind of proof someone needs to shove it in his face. But I know Grant. I know how he operates, and Leslie Anne has been slowly changing everything about herself. The way she dresses. The way she does her hair."

"Leslie Anne is his alibi for Friday night, but he specifically told Weston that nothing happened between them until that night. That he couldn't do that to you."

"Bullshit," Odessa said. "Think about it for a second. For years, he used Brown Technologies for all his IT stuff. That was the company his father used and they are reputable. Bradley took over for his dad about ten years ago and he's expanded. He's one of the best in the business. Why would Grant fire Bradley and hire Leslie Anne? Her company was new. She didn't have many clients. She wasn't a known person in the industry."

Thane pulled open the passenger door of his truck. "How long did you know about Grant and Leslie Anne?"

"I suspected the last couple of months." She climbed up in the cab with her heart in her throat, unable to look at Thane. Shame filled her soul like the rising tide.

"Why did you stay with him?" Thane said under his breath before shutting the door and jogging around the front of the truck. Once behind the steering wheel, he sighed. "I'm sorry. I just don't understand. I know I shouldn't push or judge or say a single word just because you got your memory back. You've been through hell and the last thing you need is me jumping down your throat."

She reached out and curled her fingers around his biceps. "I don't have a good reason for staying. I can't explain it without sounding like a fool. Or feeling like one."

Thane pressed the start button and revved the truck engine. It roared like a lion. "You're not a fool and I don't mean to make you feel that way." He pulled out of the parking lot and headed back toward the small neighborhood outside of town.

"You know I remember everything about my life," she said softly. "Including when I broke up with Grant the last time."

Quickly, Thane glanced in her direction with an arched brow. "What does that have to do with Leslie Anne and what we were talking about five minutes ago?"

"Leslie Anne's company took over for Bradley's about that time. I was living in my parents' house, but Grant was pushing me to sell and move in with him."

"I remember." Thane nodded. "And you sold it during that week we spent together."

"No. Grant sold it." She glanced out the window, twisting her hair. "Bradley was insulted by what Grant did. But he didn't need the business. Leslie Anne, on the other hand, well, that was her first big gig. It pretty much put her on the map. Grant told me he gave her the job because he felt bad for what she'd gone through."

"You're talking about her divorce?" Thane flipped on the blinker and turned down his mother's street. "I heard the settlement she got from that was over a million."

"It was." Odessa nodded. "But money doesn't make up for having your husband leave you for another woman." She waggled her finger. "Not everyone can have an ex-wife who is honest about what they want in a marriage and asks for it before cheating."

Thane laughed. "Yeah, Tonia is something special."

"You broke my heart when you married her." Odessa hadn't meant to blurt that out.

"And you broke mine when you went back to Grant." Thane pulled into the driveway. "We've got only a couple of minutes before we have to put on a good act for the listening devices. So was there a point to this Leslie Anne thing?"

"Yeah." Odessa nodded. "Is anyone looking into her finances? What she's done with her investments lately? Her bank accounts? Who's listed in her business? Does Grant have anything to do with it? Better yet, is anyone looking at Grant's money situation?"

Thane took her chin with his thumb and forefinger. "Yes to all of it." He leaned in and brushed his lips firmly across her mouth. It sent a hot shiver down her spine. It was the kind of heat that made a woman's clothes magically fall off her body. From the very first kiss they'd ever shared at the ripe old age of thirteen, he'd always been a magical kisser. Tender. Loving. Passionate.

This was no different.

His tongue grabbed a hold of hers, swirling. Twisting. If she allowed herself, she could get lost right here in this moment. She'd never have to return. Never have to face reality.

But what good would that do her?

She pressed her hand against his chest. Her breath hitched. She was caught somewhere between wanting to be lost in his arms.

And throttling him for being the man he'd

always been. A good man with a strong sense of right and wrong and a bigger need to right the wrongs.

"You're looking into my finances too, aren't you?" she whispered.

"No, actually, I'm not." He ran his thumb across his cheek. "If you hadn't regained your memory, I would have. But now I can ask you that question."

"Why haven't you—asked that is?"

"I didn't want to do so in front of my mother," he said softly. "You know I don't keep secrets from her, but that's your business, not mine or my mom's. I didn't want to upset you and you've only been out of the hospital for less than a day. Had your memories back less than that. I don't want to overwhelm you."

"But you'll shove your tongue in my—"

He pressed his finger over her lips. "Don't make that disgusting and don't pick a fight with me because you're upset over something that has nothing to do with me." He cocked a brow. "You know I can't stand Grant. I haven't since middle school. He's an arrogant prick. But I think he's worse than that. I think he had a hand in what happened to Chrissy and Sylvia. Rufus doesn't want to believe it—and frankly, I understand why. Weston and Haven have to straddle the line between being a cop and what information they can actually feed me. Another thing I totally accept. But right now, I'm struggling with why you're waffling. We know he's trying to paint you as a violent person. He's lied about text messages that you never sent him. Somehow, the engagement ring that you gave back to him managed to end up at the crime scene." He lowered his chin. "I don't understand why you're mad at me."

She sucked in a deep breath and let it out slowly. "It's not that I'm angry with you."

"Then what is it?"

"When I came to you months ago, I never expected to sleep with you, much—"

"Are you kidding me?"

"All right. Maybe I did. But you jumped right to relationship mode and told me you loved me. That you would always love me. That was too much. I didn't know what to do with that."

"It didn't matter because you went back to Grant." Thane dropped his hand. "I won't ever regret loving you. I'm sorry that my timing sucked. I agree I was out of line."

"And I was using you."

"I'm aware." He palmed her cheek. "It's all in the past. All that matters now is figuring out what happened."

"Did you know that no one lives in my parents' house," she said softly.

"I did notice it was empty. But I figured maybe they were going to do some remodeling."

"I asked Grant a few times about who bought it, but he's blown me off. So has the real estate agent."

Thane took her hand and kissed the inside of her palm. "I'll ask Lincoln and his wife to look into it."

Odessa bit back another sob. She hated crying. Before she let Grant into her life, she was a strong, independent woman. She made decisions for herself. She lived her life without reservation. Without apprehension. While she knew crying didn't make her weak, it felt as though it had become a way of life the last few months. As if all she had were the tears on her pillow. "I never wanted to sell. I told him that. I told him I would break up with him if he listed it and he went behind my back while I was with you and did it anyway."

"Oh, now I know why you're mad at me."

"No, Thane. I don't blame you." She grabbed his arm. "He was going to sell the house from under me whether I left him or not. I just gave him the opportunity because I was staying here with you."

Thane cupped her face and held her gaze. "I'm not going to let him hurt you ever again."

"Are you going to kiss me again?"

He smiled. "I want to, but Jett's across the street staring at us and we do need to go inside and feed wrong-ish information to Grant before Lincoln shows up." He glanced at his watch. "In forty minutes."

"Before we go inside, I want to thank you."

"There's no need for that."

"But there is." She ran her hand down the side of his face. "I haven't been very nice to you since I went back to Grant."

"No, but in all fairness, if I were him, I wouldn't necessarily support you being kind to me or hanging out with me either."

"Maybe not. However, you wouldn't forbid it." She leaned in and kissed him tenderly. It was short. Nothing special. But she'd been the one to initiate it and there was intent behind it.

That mattered. At least to her.

"That's true," he said softly. "Are you going to be okay doing this?"

"I've never been more sure about anything in

my life." And she wasn't lying about that either. Not anymore. She was ready to take down the man who had destroyed the woman she'd dreamed of becoming. The woman she planned on rebuilding.

The woman she wanted to be for herself.

And for Thane.

If he still loved her and if that kiss was real.

10

Thane leaned against the deck railing and sipped his beer. He stared at the low-hanging moon, shining bright in the star-filled sky. It was a beautiful evening. It wasn't too hot, nor was it humid. A slight breeze rippled across the air, bringing with it all the scents of summer. It was fresh. Floral. With a dash of rugged tossed in for good measure.

"You're deep in thought." Odessa's sweet voice cut through the open space. It landed on his ears like decadent chocolate melting over a graham cracker. "Did I say something wrong?"

"No, babe. You were great." He set his beer aside, inched closer, and wrapped his arm around her body. He'd been in awe of how she handled herself the second they walked in the door. The way she directed the conversation. How she mentioned she remembered everything about that night, without saying what happened.

She dropped Grant's name three times, but she didn't say he did anything. However, she tossed his name at precisely the right moment. He'd believe every word if he didn't know she was acting.

He had to admit, that freaked him right the fuck out.

He pressed his lips against her temple and inhaled sharply. She smelled like a mix of peaches and coconut. It was intoxicating. He missed that scent.

He missed her.

"My insides haven't stopped trembling." She dropped her head on his shoulder. "Reading some of the fake texts I supposedly sent made me realize how insane Grant really is. That he could be capable of… of…"

"I know." Thane hugged her closer. "Lincoln is inside making sure the last of the information we want fed to Grant is done. The police department contracted Stormi to deal with Grant's phone. She'll prove you didn't send those messages within the hour. And the warrant covers a lot of ground, so she can dig pretty deep into his computer system." He waved his hand toward the house. "That means she could be homing in on those listening devices as we speak."

"Is that what Lincoln's doing now? Helping her with that?"

"No. But he's sitting in my living room chatting on the phone with her, putting the final touches on our plan. When they are done, Grant should be worried about what we and the cops know."

"Right now, we don't know much."

"Either Grant is going to lose his shit and fuck up, leading us to what we need to know or—"

"I don't want to know the or."

"It's going to be okay," Thane whispered. "I'm going to protect you. We will get to the bottom of this. And Grant will pay for whatever crimes he's committed."

"I fear he's worse than I thought." She leaned into Thane's strong frame. Loving him had been easy. He'd been her best friend. Her confidant. The one person who understood everything about her, maybe even better than she did.

Letting him go had been the hardest thing she'd ever done. They'd been so young and Thane only eighteen when he joined the Marines. He hadn't a clue as to what he wanted to do or be. He thought the military would give him direction.

He had no idea it would give him passion.

She'd been thrilled that he found his calling. A career that stuck to him like a second skin. No way could she stand in the way of that. He'd resent her in the end if she did. But a few years and two Marine bases later, Odessa realized as much as she loved him, she resented the lifestyle. She didn't hate the military. No. She valued it. Respected it. But no fucking way could she live within its boundaries. Not at twenty.

She wasn't mature enough.

And she hadn't found her own calling. She hadn't a clue as to who she was or what she wanted.

So, she dropped out of college, broke up with Thane, and went to Europe for a year. It had to be one the best—and worst—years of her life. When she returned, she went straight to the base Thane had been stationed at and begged for him to take her back.

The next two years was more heartache. She would visit Thane, and he would come to Fallport. But she couldn't commit to moving because if she did, that meant she would be alone. Thane was already working for a special unit. He was deployed half the year. Odessa was insanely proud.

And at the same time, depressed, lonely, and needed something else out of her life.

Once again, she called it quits.

At twenty-six, they tried again.

Same thing.

By the time Thane was twenty-nine, he brought home a twenty-one-year-old. A year later, he was married. The worst part was Odessa could tell he truly loved Tonia.

And they were happy.

Odessa had to wonder if they would still be together if Tonia hadn't wanted something different from their sex life.

That stung.

"Hey." He tipped her chin with his thumb. "What's going on in that pretty little head of yours."

"You don't want to know."

He kissed the tip of her nose. "Yeah, I do."

"A world of regret." She tilted her head. "I picked the right man the first time, but I couldn't commit to your world. I thought I could after spending time abroad, but—"

He pressed his mouth over hers. His tongue

swirled around hers like a wild tornado before abruptly breaking off the kiss. "We were young and I didn't make it easy on you. I all but demanded you leave the comforts of home."

"Maybe, but it hurt more when you brought home a young girlfriend."

"I'm sure it did," he said. "But in my defense, you were dating someone at the time and I knew it before I even took out Tonia." He tucked a piece of her hair behind her ear. "The past is just that. The past. We can't change it. It's a part of who we are and we both hurt each other. I'm sorry that I was so lost. That sticking around this town wasn't something I could do at eighteen. But if I had, I would have been miserable, and I suspect we would have broken up anyway. We weren't ready for each other."

"Now you sound like my therap…" She took a step back, pressing her hand on the center of his chest. "We need to get a couple of my therapy sessions to the police."

"Excuse me?" Thane held her stare. "What does that have to do with anything?"

"I started seeing a therapist before my parents died. I struggled with getting my life on track." She covered his mouth. It killed him that he had anything to do with any negativity in her life. But he'd keep his thoughts to himself if that's what she wanted. "When my folks died in that car crash, I felt so alone. Your mom was great, but it wasn't you."

"I called. I came home. You shut me out." Thane didn't want to have this conversation. He feared it would lead to a fight. One that he never wanted to have. It no longer mattered. He understood more than he wanted. He also forgave Odessa.

He loved her and what he wanted was for her to get her life back.

While he wanted to be in her life as more than a friend, he would take her as a friend because that was better than nothing.

"I know and that was because of Grant," she said. "I didn't expect you to comfort me, even though that's who I wanted. Maybe even who I needed. I spoke with my therapist about it. She was all about me making a decision. You were a free man. Divorced and not dating anyone. I wasn't dating Grant yet. But he'd made it very clear what he wanted. He showered me with gifts. He was always there for me. He was really sweet in the beginning. Too bad it was all an act."

"I don't mean to be an asshole, but I'm really glad to hear you say that about that jerk off."

She chuckled. It wasn't really funny, but she appreciated the sentiment. "Anyway, I continued to see that therapist for months. I talked a lot about my conflicting feelings about you leaving the military—knowing you were going to move back. About dating Grant and how much you hated him and how I struggled to understand the pull he had on me."

"What did the therapist have to say?"

"That is what's interesting to me," Odessa said. "In the beginning, she mostly listened. She prescribed me antidepressants when my folks died. However, I didn't like the way they made me feel and after a few months, I stopped taking them. Grant tried to push them on me, but I couldn't bring myself to take them."

"They aren't for everyone," he said. "Why did you stop seeing the therapist? Did Grant make you?"

"You know, outside of the 'happy pills,' as Grant called them, he thought seeing a shrink was weak. That's what he told me. When he knew I was going, he'd tell me I should cancel and take up golf or tennis and stay away from you. That those things would make me happy. That and lose ten pounds, change my hair color, among other things."

"I really hate that man," Thane muttered.

"Thing is, he never flat-out demanded I stop. But slowly, my therapist encouraged me to choose. She told me it wasn't fair to lead Grant on. But she never once mentioned what it was or could be doing to you. And I was texting with you. We saw each other often when you first moved here. And she knew all that. Instead, she focused on what I was doing to the man who was taking care of me."

"I can't believe I'm going to say this, because again, I despise Grant, but that therapist does have a point. I mean, if I were in Grant's shoes, I might actually be jealous, and I'm not a jealous man. But that might give me a reason to be. Especially with our history." He smoothed his hands down her back, cupping her ass, heaving her close to his chest to prove a point.

"I get it. But I stopped seeing her not because anyone asked me to, but because I didn't feel like I was getting anything out of it. I felt as though I had been pushed into a relationship with Grant. That I was being pushed into moving out of my parents' home. Into selling it."

"Wait a second." Thane took a step back and

raked his fingers through his hair. "If that's the case, why did you call and schedule an appointment?"

"I didn't, Thane." She pursed her lips. "At least I don't remember doing it and I have most of those memories back."

Thane yanked his cell from his back pocket. He had two calls to make. The first one might not go over too well. He tapped his screen and hit the speaker button.

"You're calling Jenna?" Odessa glanced between him and the phone.

He didn't get a chance to answer.

"Why the hell are you calling me so late?" Jenna asked. "Is Odessa okay?"

"She's fine," Thane said. "She's standing right here. You're on speaker."

"Oh. Okay. What's up?" Jenna asked, a little calmer.

Thane arched a brow. He had a few fatal flaws. One of them was something he hated Grant for being: controlling. Another one was he tended to speak for others.

In this moment, he combined his two worst traits together. It didn't matter that he'd done so because he loved and adored Odessa. Nope. But it could backfire.

She nodded, as if she understood his thoughts. "I didn't make that appointment with Doctor Borden. If I were to go back to seeing a therapist, I'd go to anyone but her."

"Why?" Jenna asked. "She's got a good reputation."

"That may be true. But I don't believe she had my best interests at heart during my sessions and I want to know if we can get her notes," Odessa said.

"I've already asked for them. But I figured she and I would sit down and have a discussion."

"That's probably not going to happen." Odessa sighed, leaning against the railing. "A few months ago, I remember seeing the good doctor with Heath, and they looked awfully cozy."

"Where and what exactly do you mean by cozy?" Thane asked.

"In the parking lot by her office and kissy-face cozy." Odessa folded her arms. "Why would Grant target me from the beginning?"

"The insurance money. The house," Thane said, as if that were obvious. "He had a crush on you in middle school. He made his move and it backfired."

"I embarrassed him." Odessa closed her eyes.

Thane inched closer. They'd been in the seventh

grade. She was madly in love with Thane. And Thane with her. It was time.

But Thane couldn't do a grand gesture. She wouldn't appreciate that, so he opted for something a little less subtle. A simple note in her locker to meet him under the bleachers at lunch where they shared their first kiss.

It had been magical.

Then Grant happened.

"Childhood trauma can often shape a person's life," Jenna said.

"I'm not responsible for that man's cruelty." Odessa blinked.

"That's not what I'm saying, although it might help if I knew what happened," Jenna said.

"In a nutshell, Grant purchased a dozen roses from the secret admirer Valentine's Day thing we did every year." Thane rubbed the back of his neck. He couldn't believe they were even discussing this stupid story. "He even made a mixed tape of what he believed were her favorite songs. He didn't even come close to the music she liked. I mean, first, she wasn't the kind of girl who wanted a secret admirer. And Grant couldn't have known we'd already kissed earlier that day. So, when the roses started coming, and she knew they weren't from me, she simply dumped them in the trash. When the mixed tape was played with a dedication over the loudspeaker for the entire school to hear, she stood up on her chair and made it clear that whoever sent it didn't know her at all and to leave her the fuck alone. That she had a boyfriend and his name was Thane. Her exact words. She hopped off her chair and kissed me so hard in front of everyone that I too was embarrassed."

"Like hell you were."

"Okay, so maybe I wasn't." Thane laughed. "But Grant was in the room. He heard her and saw us. But to his credit, he didn't say a word and acted like it wasn't him."

"Dumb question here," Jenna said. "If the roses were anonymous and so was the tape, how did you know it was Grant?"

Thane took Odessa into his arms, kissing her temple. "Chrissy was our class president. She handled the secret admirer stuff every year. She knew it was Grant."

Odessa sniffled. "Unfortunately, when Chrissy told me, I got in Grant's face. Called him a loser and told him I'd never in a million years ever go out with him." She dropped her head to Thane's shoulder.

"That's only because he wouldn't stop sending you secret admirer gifts with notes that said nasty things about me," Grant said.

"That's a weak motive, but stranger things have happened," Jenna said.

"Yeah, but let's not forget what Rufus said. The man might be broke, which means he's going after people who have money," Thane said. "Sticking it to Odessa—which is also hurting me—is icing on the cake."

"I'm supposed to see Doctor Borden in the morning. I'll—"

"I don't want you anywhere near that doctor alone," Thane interrupted Jenna. "Request the files. If she doesn't hand them over or if you need a face-to-face, let me know. I'll send someone or have Weston send a cop over."

"Thanks. I won't say no," Jenna said. "I'll call you tomorrow. Have a good night."

Thane tapped the screen. He took Odessa's hand.

Just then, Lincoln strolled through the sliding glass doors, waving his cell. "I've got Weston and my wife on the line," he said. "Stormi found some shit on Grant's computer." Lincoln held his tablet in his hands. He set it on the small table and waved everyone over. "First, Stormi can prove without a doubt, those texts were not what Odessa sent on Friday night. As a matter of fact, here's the text string."

Thane rested his hand on Odessa's shoulder and leaned forward, squinting as he read nasty words on the screen.

You're going to pay for leaving me.

Only that wasn't from Odessa. It was from Grant.

You better come home, or I'm coming for you.

Bitch, who you do you think you are.

Answer your fucking phone if you know what's good for you.

I'm tired of this game. I've been good to you. I've let you have your tantrum. Come home, or else.

You want to play this game. Fine. I'll play. But others will suffer. He'll suffer. Your girlfriends, they will suffer.

"Jesus. That's fucking threatening as hell," Thane whispered.

"It's enough for me to bring him in for questioning," Weston said. "But there's more."

"What kind of more?" Thane asked.

Lincoln tapped his fingers across his tablet. "Grant's broke and he has a coke problem. I've isolated texts messages from someone by the name of Tito Vargas, a major drug dealer who Grant owes a lot of money to. Grant could pay off his debts with the scam he's running with Leslie Anne."

"I don't like her, but I feel bad she's falling for the same crap I did," Odessa said.

"That's not the bigger problem." Lincoln tapped his finger. "A month ago, Grant took out a life insurance policy on Odessa for the amount of five million dollars."

"He did what?" Odessa jerked upright. "Are you trying to tell me he's been planning on killing me?"

"Unfortunately." Lincoln nodded. "But his plan didn't include your friends. Nor did he plan on doing it this past weekend. However, since you left him, he had to scramble. And he's continuing to shift his plans. But he's as a dumb as a motherfucking doornail because he's left a trail."

"What kind of trail?" Thane asked.

"Look at these emails he's sent to Heath, the man he's hired to do his dirty work." Lincoln shook his head. "Not only is he a moron for communicating with a hired hitman this way, but he's a fool if he actually thinks a plan like this would work now."

Thane reached around Lincoln and lifted the tablet. "That depends on what Odessa's previous therapist has in her notes about Odessa's sessions." He lifted his gaze and let out a long breath. "And that doctor—we believe—is fucking Heath."

"No shit," Lincoln said. "Well, then I suppose making you out to be homicidal and suicidal in one breath might not be a stretch."

Thane turned and stared through the sliding glass doors. "We need to end this. Tonight."

"I've got all I need to bring both Grant and Heath in," Weston said over the phone's speaker. "But they won't talk. They will lawyer up and even though I'm fairly confident I can charge them both with crimes, they will be out of this station in twenty-four hours. It's then up to—"

"I know how the court system works and we're not going to do that." Thane rolled his shoulders. "We're going to make sure Grant and Heath make an appearance. Here. Tonight. We're going to have them come for her." He swallowed the bile that smacked his tonsils. It tasted like death. He shifted his stance and stared at Odessa.

Her eyes were wide with fear. But there was also a strength behind those baby blues. A resolve. A desire to end this and get her life back.

"We're going to go inside and give them a reason to storm my house tonight. We've already hinted that she knows. That she remembers what happened." Thane pointed toward the tablet. "Now we're going to toss some of their plan right back in their faces. We're going to push their buttons and give them no other choice. And then we're going to be ready to take them down. I want this conviction to stick. I don't want there to be any doubt and Grant is just arrogant enough to look me in the eye and let me know he finally beat me."

"Are you sure?" Lincoln asked. "Because you're putting Odessa at risk."

"I know." Thane nodded. He closed the gap between him and Odessa. He cupped her face. "I'm asking a lot of you. I know you're scared. I'm afraid too. I know men like Heath. They believe they are invincible. Worse, they don't have a moral compass. But if we don't get them to charge—"

"I'm all in," she said, squaring her shoulders. "I'd rather this than take the risk he beats the system."

"That's my girl." Thane brushed his lips across her mouth.

"All right. I'll get the ball rolling and see who's available for a good old-fashioned sting op," Lincoln said.

"I can redirect the listening devices to the police

station," Stormi said. "Lucky us, Virginia is a one-party consent state, making all of this fun stuff legal. Talk to you boys in a bit. Honey, I'll see you at home when this is over."

"Kiss the kiddies for me," Lincoln said. "This should be an easy enough plan, but I do have a question for you."

"Yeah. What's that?" Thane asked.

"What about Rufus?" Lincoln arched a brow. "You say he's no longer a part of this and the bugs were exactly where he said they were. But how do we deal with him if we can't contact him?"

"I left him a burner phone, and he took it. I'll reach out to him on that." Thane lifted his cell and texted the number of the burner. "Hopefully, he'll call soon. I'll fill him in and he can be our inside man."

"I hope you're right because if not, we're fucked." Lincoln tucked his tablet under his arm and disappeared inside.

"Before we move forward, I need to say a couple of things." Thane ran his thumb across Odessa's cheek.

"Me first."

"Okay." He lowered his chin. "I'm all ears."

She took his hand and placed it over her heart.

"I know how you feel about me. I suspect what you want to say is that you love me. That you always have and that you always will."

"That's part of it," he admitted. "But you say that as if it's a side note and it's not."

She opened her mouth.

He hushed her with his index finger. "I love you. I want us to date when this is over. To have a second chance at falling in love again. I know you're going to need time. Your life hasn't been easy this last year."

"Neither has yours," she said. "You left the only career you've ever had. You lost your father and you've been taking care of your mom." She palmed his cheek. "I don't need time. What I need is you."

"That you have."

"Good, because I do still love you." She kissed him tenderly. "However, you are right. We do need to date." She smiled. "Falling in love again will be fun. Now let's go take out the fucking trash."

"You've always had a way with words."

11

Odessa hated waiting. It didn't matter that she knew a small army had gathered around Thane's house. Or that they'd been told Grant had left his house.

The seconds ticked by in what seemed like hours.

She sat on the sofa, watching some dumbass movie, snuggling into Thane's strong body. But it didn't help. Not one bit. All she could think about was all the things that could go wrong.

Thane and Odessa had spoken openly about some of the intel they had come across, though they hadn't mentioned how they got it. They discussed how they knew about Leslie Anne. About how he'd stolen money from Odessa and taken out a life insurance policy.

They had her admit that she never scheduled the therapy session and that she saw Heath and her doctor.

It was all a game to get Grant to Thane's front door.

But did it work?

It had to.

Grant would need to get rid of those who threatened him.

Thane leaned forward and scribbled on a piece of paper, resting it on her knee.

Grant is pulling into the neighborhood. Heath and Rufus are with him. Remember what we talked about. Follow my lead and if they pull a gun, you stay behind me. Do not make me push you to the ground.

Thane cocked his head.

She nodded.

He wadded up the paper and tossed it into the fireplace. Then he removed his earpiece. Five minutes later, the front doorbell rang.

Odessa's heart dropped to her feet like a cement brick. She thought she was ready for this. But she wasn't. She wanted to crawl under the sofa and hide.

You can't hide from me, Odessa. I'll find you. And I'll finish you.

Those words. That voice.

She rubbed her neck.

Flashes of Heath showing up at the campsite and interrupting her and her friends. He'd come to collect her. To bring her back, even if he had to take her kicking and screaming.

Or better yet, drugging her.

"It was Heath," she whispered, clutching Thane's shoulders. "He was the one who came to the campsite. He was dressed as a park ranger." She swallowed. "I was at the bathroom. We'd all been fighting over the texts and how I should handle them. I saw him. I saw Heath. He killed—"

"Shhhh, babe." Thane turned and held her by the forearms. "I'm so sorry this is all coming back right now," he whispered against her cheek. "Can you hold it together for a little while longer?"

"Yes, but there are things that you need to know about that night… that Weston needs to know."

"Feel free to improvise when you see the right moment." He kissed her cheek, turned, and opened the door where she came face-to-face with the man who killed her friends.

And the man who came back and tried to finish the job.

"What the fuck are you doing here?" Thane didn't have to fake his disgust. Hearing the tremble in Odessa's voice a moment ago rattled Thane's resolve.

Making her face down the men who killed her friends was one thing, but now that she remembered the gruesome scene—Thane wanted to kick himself. How cruel.

Grant didn't waste any time showing his hand. He pulled out a weapon, and so did Heath. "I'd let me in if I were you and I wouldn't try anything funny." Grant jerked his free hand over his shoulder. "I've got a few other friends with me. Tell your buddy across the street to stand down."

Thane stared at Rufus, who held a weapon at Jett. "Take a hike, Jett," Thane called. "We're fine."

"Are you sure?" Jett called.

"I'm sure."

This had all been expected. However, Thane wished it was Rufus on his front porch, not Heath.

But as long as Rufus was on his side, things should work out fine.

It meant Rufus could redirect the other men that Grant brought, giving Thane's men the upper hand.

Thane just needed to give everyone enough time to do it.

"Now let us in." Grant didn't wait for Thane to step aside; he muscled himself across the threshold, shoving Odessa aside.

"Fucking touch her again, and I'll kill you with my bare hands." Thane sidestepped Grant and tugged Odessa close.

"No, you won't." Grant laughed. "Ever since we were kids, you've acted like you were better than me. As if your shit doesn't stink. Like some holier-than-thou asshole." Grant raised his weapon, aiming it dead center at Thane's chest.

At least it wasn't toward Odessa.

But Thane didn't expect this to go south so quickly. Now that it did, he might as well go for the jugular.

He stepped in front of Odessa.

Heath strolled around the family room and into the kitchen as if looking for something. Or some-one. Well, he wasn't going to find the listening devices. And none of Thane's buddies were inside the house.

Not yet anyway.

If things went according to plan, someone would be climbing through the upstairs window once the outside was secure.

"You know what, Grant? It's because I am better. At everything. You sucked at football. You had to buy your way into college. You had to manipulate to get Odessa to give you the time of day, and then to keep her, you had to kill."

Grant laughed, a full-on hard belly laugh. "Only, I don't want to keep her anymore. She's too much fucking work. Not worth the effort." Grant leaned forward. "She's not even a good fuck."

Thane would not be goaded into the response that Grant wanted. But Thane would give him a response. "Maybe that's because you don't know how to satisfy a real woman."

Grant charged forward. He raised his weapon and smacked Thane across the face.

Crack! Thud.

Thane groaned.

Odessa stifled a scream.

Blood dripped down the cut on Thane's cheek. He wiped his face. "Does that make you feel like a man?" Thane squared his shoulders, preparing for another blow. As long as he didn't get trigger happy, he'd take a few punches.

"I'm more man than you'll ever be." Grant shifted his stance. He pressed the hard metal into Thane's gut. "Have you found all those bugs yet?"

"They aren't where—"

"That's because I found them." Thane waggled his brows and smiled. "They're obviously still in the house because you've been listening, but I moved them."

Grant's mouth drew into a tight line. "So, tell me, how much of your conversation was a ruse to get me over here, and what was the truth?"

"Babe, would you like the honors?" Thane wasn't sure he should give her the floor. But if she didn't want it, or couldn't take it, he'd deal with the situation. He'd make sure Grant paid.

That he'd spend the rest of his life in prison.

While Thane spent the rest of his making sure Odessa knew at least one person loved and adored her.

12

That night swam in Odessa's brain like a drowning rat. It played over and over again. Each time, the images became sharper. More defined. Even the drug-induced haze when she'd woken up after racing off in the darkness was a memory she'd never forget again.

"I remember everything," Odessa said with more strength in her voice than she thought she'd ever have again when facing down Grant. "I watched that man stab my friends. I came back from the bathroom and saw him with the knife and blood on his hands."

"Now you're talking crazy shit," Heath said.

"You think I can't remember because I was

drunk and drugged? But I do," Odessa said. "I felt you stick me with that needle. I remember kicking you. Fighting you. I ran off, and I hid in the woods, where I watched you toss my friends over the cliff." Odessa eased out from behind Thane's body. She held Grant's steely-eyed glare. She'd never seen his eyes so wild and out of control before. She inched back behind Thane.

What kind of coward was she?

She swallowed.

"But it was you, Grant, who called my name in the darkness. It was you who came back for me. You were going to finish the job, weren't you."

Grant shrugged. "I'm here, aren't I?"

"You won't get away with it," Thane said. "You can't kill us. People will ask questions. It will be too convoluted."

"Is this where you think I will tell you my plan?" Grant asked.

"No," Odessa asked. "That wouldn't be as much fun as informing you that I already know your plan and how it won't work."

"You're a stupid bitch. You don't know shit." Grant waved his gun. "Heath, I'm done with these two."

"But, boss, the bugs. How do we know they didn't set them up to—"

"Leslie Anne would have known if they had been redirected. And she would have told me. She's loyal to me," Grant said.

Odessa knew very little about technology. However, she did trust Lincoln and his wife. If there was any chance Leslie Anne could have figured out someone else was using their device to listen, they wouldn't have done it.

"I'm not worried," Grant said. "Get a hold of Rufus and make sure there aren't any surprises outside. Once we know that, I'll be out that door and you can handle these two idiots."

Odessa's heart pounded. Thane just stood there. He didn't move a muscle. He didn't turn his head. He didn't say a word. She had no idea if that was good or bad. This whole thing felt like it went down too fast. And she wasn't even sure if Grant had said enough. He never actually admitted to anything.

"Boss, we've got a problem," Heath said.

"What's that?" Grant asked.

"You're not going to like it." Heath stomped across the room. "Leslie Anne just texted. It appears Stacey Wilkerson just came on the air with breaking news regarding the murders."

"And?" Grant held his weapon pointed right at Thane.

"The cops believe they know who killed those girls, but the people in question are holding someone hostage." Health held his phone up.

"What the fuck have you done to me, Odessa?" Grant reached out and snagged her by the hair.

"Let her—"

Bang!

"No!" Odessa screamed.

Thane clutched his gut. He dropped to his knees. A searing pain ripped through his body. Blood poured between his fingertips. It was hot and flowed like a raging river.

Getting shot was not part of the plan.

Stacey reporting on anything was not part of the plan.

How the fuck did she find out?

"You shot him," Odessa whispered. "He needs an ambulance."

"I'm getting the fuck out of here," Heath said. "You blew it, Grant. You're on your own now. Even I can't help you with this one."

"Oh, yes, you can." Grant shifted his weapon, pointing it at Heath while he still had a death grip on Odessa.

Thane rocked back on his heels. The pain faded into the background. His body went numb. Having been shot before, he knew that wasn't good. He also knew he didn't have much time. He was losing too much blood.

A shadow by the corner of the kitchen caught his attention.

But he couldn't make it out. Was it a person or a figment of his dying imagination?

God, he wanted to lie down and close his eyes.

"Do not point that thing at me." Heath raised his weapon. "I will kill you and not think twice. I will turn on you and tell the cops whatever they need to hear to put you away and save my own ass."

Thane believed that one. About both men.

The shadow moved and before he realized what was happening, Rufus jumped on Heath. Or maybe pushed him out of the way. Thane couldn't be sure.

Bang!

Odessa screamed before her body covered Thane, shoving him completely to the floor.

Damn, that hurt.

The front door flew open.

"Drop your weapon, Grant," Weston's voice bellowed. "You're under arrest."

"We need an ambulance." Odessa ripped off her shirt and pressed it over Thane's wound.

"Please put that back on," he managed to gurgle out. "I haven't seen those in a while and I don't like all my buddies—"

"Stop talking." Odessa covered his mouth. "You're barely making sense anyway."

"Yes, ma'am." He sighed. The clambering of feet rattled the floorboards. Rufus stood over him, holding his arm as blood dripped down his biceps. "Sorry I couldn't get inside sooner."

"Sorry you got shot," Thane whispered.

Rufus shrugged. "Flesh wound." He waggled his finger. "You better not die on me. I'm going to need a friend."

"I'll try not to." But Thane honestly wasn't sure. He could feel his pulse slow.

Odessa palmed his cheek. "I'm going to have words with whoever told Stacey about our plan."

"That would have been me, ma'am," Heath said as Weston slapped the cuffs on his wrists. "It was the only way I could think of to get out from under that asshole."

"You're a fucking traitor," Grant yelled as another police officer tugged him out the door.

Thane tried to process the words, but everything was so hazy. And he was so damn tired.

Stay awake. Don't sleep. He knew the drill.

"What? I don't understand," Odessa said.

"I'm sorry we couldn't tell the two of you." Weston pressed his hand over hers, adding more pressure to Thane's gut.

He groaned.

"Tell us what?" Odessa asked.

"Right before all this went down, Stormi got a cryptic message from Heath. Turns out, Grant was blackmailing him and Doctor Borden. Heath's willing to turn on Grant," Weston said. "Even though it might cost him his freedom."

"I know I'm not a good guy. But that asshole is worse. I'm willing to do my time for my crimes as long as that guy goes down for all the shit he's done and I'm willing to turn it all over," Heath said.

"I think we all are," Rufus added.

Thane was grateful for that. Odessa would be free to live her life. Nothing was standing in her way now. He tried to suck in a deep breath but couldn't.

"EMTs are here," someone said. "Let's make room and let these guys get to work."

That was Thane's cue to really let go.

He found Odessa's hand, turned his head, and smiled.

"I love you too," she said. "Now fight like you would expect me to."

The world went black.

13

TWO MONTHS LATER…

Odessa stood over the gravesite. "You're not going to believe it," she whispered. "I did it. I got married. To Thane." She twisted her wedding band around before tentatively reaching out and running her finger across the words on her parents' shared tombstone. "And you're going to be grandparents, but I haven't told him that yet. He's going to freak out. Like fall off his rocker, freak out. His mom knows. I couldn't keep that from her, especially since her illness is getting worse. I fear she doesn't have too much longer with us." She glanced over her shoulder, smiled, and waved at her handsome husband who strolled down the path.

He nearly died two months ago.

She would have never forgiven herself if that happened.

But all was right in the world.

Rufus had his company back and was doing well. Some people didn't trust him, but given time, that would change. And he was dating.

Leslie Anne, of all people.

But she was a victim like everyone else.

And, as it turned it, was super sweet.

Go figure.

Heath, well, he was in prison. The judge was lenient, and eventually, he'd get out. And thanks to Heath, Grant was sentenced to prison for the rest of his life without the possibility of parole. His crimes went much further than they had initially thought, and Rufus and Heath made sure the cops had what they needed.

"Hey, babe, sorry I'm late." Thane leaned in and kissed her cheek. "Having a nice visit?"

"I am. How did things go with your mom at the doctor's?"

Thane ran a hand across his mouth. "Not that great and she's being super stubborn about selling the house. But she knows we have to. She can't do stairs anymore."

"Did you tell her I got my parents' house back?"

When Thane learned that Grant had sold her house to an LLC who intended on renovating and renting, he jumped through hoops to buy it back. At first, it was annoying, but only because she wanted to buy it herself. To be independent. But she realized being in a relationship with Thane—being married to him—didn't take away from her independence at all. If anything, he gave her back her freedom.

Thane nodded. "That knowledge and the fact that it's got a bedroom on the first floor for her is the only reason she's agreeing to letting me put the family home up for sale. Though, I did have to call Asher."

"Ouch. Both her boys ganging up on her. That's not nice. And here I thought I was going to have to pull out the grandparent card." She took his hand and placed it on her stomach.

"Haha. Only my brother can do that and it doesn't work, because her grandkids only come…" His gaze dropped to her midsection. "You're… You're… We're… We're…"

"Having trouble spitting that out?" She laughed.

"You know, my mom kept saying weird things about that one small room at the top of the stairs in your parents' house and how it would make for a great nursery." He waggled his finger under her nose. "You told my mama we're going to have a baby before you told me?"

"Of course I did." She wrapped her arms around his strong shoulders. "Are you mad?"

"Absolutely not." He kissed her nose. "I'm the happiest man on the planet. I have the best wife and now I'm going to be a... Holy shit. I'm going to be a dad. That's crazy. What the hell do I know about being a father? I'm probably going to drop the kid on its head."

"I doubt that." She smiled. "You'll figure it and you'll be great." For the first time in what felt like her entire life, Odessa knew exactly what she wanted out of life. She wasn't searching for anything. It had always been right in front of her.

ABOUT THE AUTHOR

Jen Talty is the *USA Today* Bestselling Author of Contemporary Romance, Romantic Suspense, and Paranormal Romance. In the fall of 2020, her short story was selected and featured in a 1001 Dark Nights Anthology.

Regardless of the genre, her goal is to take you on a ride that will leave you floating under the sun with warmth in your heart. She writes stories about broken heroes and heroines who aren't necessarily looking for romance, but in the end, they find the kind of love books are written about :).

She first started writing while carting her kids to one hockey rink after the other, averaging 170 games per year between 3 kids in 2 countries and 5 states. Her first book, IN TWO WEEKS was originally published in 2007. In 2010 she helped form a publishing company (Cool Gus Publishing) with *NY*

Times Bestselling Author Bob Mayer where she ran the technical side of the business through 2016.

Jen is currently enjoying the next phase of her life…the empty nester! She and her husband reside in Jupiter, Florida.

Grab a glass of vino, kick back, relax, and let the romance roll in…

Sign up for my Newsletter (https://dl.bookfunnel.com/82gm8b9k4y) where I often give away free books before publication.

Join my private Facebook group (https://www.facebook.com/groups/191706547909047/) where I post exclusive excerpts and discuss all things murder and love!

Never miss a new release. Follow me on Amazon:amazon.com/author/jentalty

And on Bookbub: bookbub.com/authors/jen-talty

Legacy Series

Dark Legacy

Legacy of Lies

Secret Legacy

Emerald City

Investigate Av

Sail Aw

Fly A ay

Fli way

Hawaii Br rhood Protectors

W n Unleashed

wie's Battle

Colo otherhood Protectors

ing For Esme

efending Raven

Fay's Six

Darius' Promise

owstone Brotherhood Protectors

Guarding Payton

Wyatt's Mission

Corbin's Mission

Candlewood Falls

Rivers Edge

The Buried Secret

Its In His Kiss

Lips Of An Angel

Kisses Sweeter than Wine

A Little Bit Whiskey

It's all in the Whiskey

Johnnie Walker

Georgia Moon

Jack Daniels

Jim Beam

Whiskey Sour

Whiskey Cobbler

Whiskey Smash

Irish Whiskey

The Monroes

Color Me Yours

Color Me Smart

Color Me Free

Color Me Lucky

Color Me Ice

Color Me Home

Search and Rescue

Protecting Ainsley

Protecting Clover

Protecting Olympia

Protecting Freedom

Protecting Princess

Protecting Marlowe

DELTA FORCE-NEXT GENERATION

Shielding Jolene

Shielding Aalyiah

Shielding Laine

Shielding Talullah

Shielding Maribel

Shielding Daisy

The Men of Thief Lake

Rekindled

Destiny's Dream

Federal Investigators

Jane Doe's Return

The Butterfly Murders

THE AEGIS NETWORK

The Sarich Brother

The Lighthouse

Her Last Hope

The Last Flight

The Return Home

The Matriarch

Aegis Network: Jacksonville Division

A SEAL's Honor

Talon's Honor

Arthur's Honor

Rex's Honor

Kent's Honor

Buddy's Honor

Aegis Network Short Stories

Max & Milian

A Christmas Miracle

Spinning Wheels

Holiday's Vacation

The Brotherhood Protectors

Out of the Wild

Rough Justice

Rough Around The Edges

Rough Ride

Rough Edge

Rough Beauty

The Brotherhood Protectors

The Saving Series

Saving Love

Saving Magnolia

Saving Leather

Hot Hunks

Cove's Blind Date Blows Up

My Everyday Hero – Ledger

Tempting Tavor

Malachi's Mystic Assignment

Needing Neor

Holiday Romances

A Christmas Getaway

Alaskan Christmas

Whispers

Christmas In The Sand

Heroes & Heroines on the Field

Taking A Risk

Tee Time

A New Dawn

The Blind Date

Spring Fling

Summers Gone

Winter Wedding

The Awakening

Fated Moons

The Collective Order

The Lost Sister

The Lost Soldier

The Lost Soul

The Lost Connection

The New Order

There are many more books in this fan fiction world than listed here, for an up-to-date list go to www.AcesPress.com

You can also visit our Amazon page at: http://www.amazon.com/author/operationalpha

Special Forces: Operation Alpha World

Christie Adams: Charity's Heart
Elizabella Baker: Challenging Luke
Linzi Baxter: Dangerous Rescue
Misha Blake: Flash
Anna Blakely: Rescuing Gracelynn
Julia Bright: Saving Lorelei
Cara Carnes: Protecting Mari
Kendra Mei Chailyn: Beast
Melissa Kay Clarke: Rescuing Annabeth
Gia Cobie: Saved from Revenge
Samantha Cole: Handling Haven
Cassie Colton: Rescuing Ryder
KaLyn Cooper: Spring Unveiled
Jordan Dane: Redemption for Avery
D.M. Earl: Claire's Guardian
Riley Edwards: Protecting Olivia
Dorothy Ewels: Knight's Queen
Lila Ferrari: Protecting Joy

Nicole Flockton: Protecting Maria
Lea Griffith: Finding Ava
Desiree Holt: Protecting Maddie
Danielle M. Haas: Crossroads of Betrayal
Bree Hera: Trusting the Team
Rayne Lewis: Justice for Mary
Kristin Lynn: Worth the Risk
JM Madden: Rescuing Olivia
A.M. Mahler: Griffin
Ellie Masters: Sybil's Protector
Trish McCallan: Hero Under Fire
Naomi McKay: Twist
KD Michaels: Saving Laura
Olivia Michaels: Protecting Harper
Annie Miller: Securing Willow
MJ Nightingale: Protecting Beauty
C.K. O'Connor: Delaney's Bodyguard
Danielle Pays: Defending Sarina
Lainey Reese: Protecting New York
Taryn Rivers: Savage Cove
TL Reeve and Michele Ryan: Extracting Mateo
Ariana Rose: Chasing Paige
Angela Rush: Charlotte
E.M. Shue: Discovering Tyler
Heather Slade: Code Name: Admiral
Dee Stewart: Fighting for Brielle

Lynne St. James: SEAL's Spitfire
Bella Stone: Rexar
Jen Talty: Protecting Ainsley
Reina Torres, Rescuing Hi'ilani
LJ Vickery: Circus Comes to Town
R. C. Wynne: Shadows Renewed

Delta Team Three Series

Lori Ryan: Nori's Delta
Becca Jameson: Destiny's Delta
Lynne St James, Gwen's Delta
Elle James: Ivy's Delta
Riley Edwards: Hope's Delta

Police and Fire: Operation Alpha World

Freya Barker: Burning for Autumn
B.P. Beth: Scott
Jane Blythe: Salvaging Marigold
Julia Bright: Justice for Amber
Gia Cobie: Saved from Revenge
Leyna Cohan: Embracing Juliette
Nicole Craig: Justice for Francesca
Danielle M. Haas: Crossroads of Betrayal
Deanndra Hall: Shelter for Sharla
India Kells: Game Master
Reina Torres: Justice for Sloane

Tarpley VFD Series

As you know, this book included at least one character from Susan Stoker's books. To check out more, see below.

SEAL of Protection: Alliance Series

Protecting Remi
Protecting Wren
Protecting Josie
Protecting Maggie (Apr 1, 2025)
Protecting Addison (May 6, 2025)
Protecting Kelli (Sept 2, 2025)
Protecting Bree (TBA)

Rescue Angels Series

Keeping Laryn (July 1, 2025)
Keeping Amanda (Nov 4, 2025)
Keeping Zita (Feb 2026)
Keeping Penny (TBA)
Keeping Kara (TBA)
Keeping Jennifer (TBA)

The Refuge Series

Deserving Alaska
Deserving Henley
Deserving Reese

Deserving Cora

Deserving Lara

Deserving Maisy

Deserving Ryleigh

SEAL Team Hawaii Series

Finding Elodie

Finding Lexie

Finding Kenna

Finding Monica

Finding Carly

Finding Ashlyn

Finding Jodelle

Eagle Point Search & Rescue

Searching for Lilly

Searching for Elsie

Searching for Bristol

Searching for Caryn

Searching for Finley

Searching for Heather

Searching for Khloe

Delta Team Two Series

Shielding Gillian

Shielding Kinley

Shielding Aspen

Shielding Jayme (novella)

Shielding Riley

Shielding Devyn

Shielding Ember

Shielding Sierra

SEAL of Protection: Legacy Series

Securing Caite (FREE!)

Securing Brenae (novella)

Securing Sidney

Securing Piper

Securing Zoey

Securing Avery

Securing Kalee

Securing Jane

Delta Force Heroes Series

Rescuing Rayne

Rescuing Aimee (novella)

Rescuing Emily

Rescuing Harley

Marrying Emily (novella)

Rescuing Kassie

Rescuing Bryn

Rescuing Casey

Rescuing Sadie (novella)
Rescuing Wendy
Rescuing Mary
Rescuing Macie (novella)
Rescuing Annie

Badge of Honor: Texas Heroes Series

Justice for Mackenzie (FREE!)
Justice for Mickie
Justice for Corrie
Justice for Laine (novella)
Shelter for Elizabeth
Justice for Boone
Shelter for Adeline
Shelter for Sophie
Justice for Erin
Justice for Milena
Shelter for Blythe
Justice for Hope
Shelter for Quinn
Shelter for Koren
Shelter for Penelope

SEAL of Protection Series

Protecting Caroline (FREE!)
Protecting Alabama

Protecting Fiona
Marrying Caroline (novella)
Protecting Summer
Protecting Cheyenne
Protecting Jessyka
Protecting Julie (novella)
Protecting Melody
Protecting the Future
Protecting Kiera (novella)
Protecting Alabama's Kids (novella)
Protecting Dakota

New York Times, *USA Today* and *Wall Street Journal* Bestselling Author Susan Stoker has a heart as big as the state of Tennessee where she lives, but this all American girl has also spent the last fourteen years living in Missouri, California, Colorado, Indiana, and Texas. She's married to a retired Army man who now gets to follow *her* around the country.

www.stokeraces.com
www.AcesPress.com
susan@stokeraces.com

Made in United States
Cleveland, OH
29 March 2025